At the end of the Summer term, Carolus Deene, amateur detective cum history master of Queen's School, Newminster, is summoned to Suffolk to investigate the circumstances attending the discovery of the body of Mrs Lillianne Bomberger, a writer of detective fiction. The body had been buried in the sand in an upright position with only the head protruding; at least one tide had been over it. Before Carolus Deene's investigations are complete his interest begins to flag, but two further bodies appear on the scene, stimulating the schoolmaster detective to pursue this "beastly case" with renewed acumen to its ultimate and bitter conclusion.

By the same Author

'Sergeant Beef' Novels:

        CASE FOR THREE DETECTIVES

        CASE WITHOUT A CORPSE

        CASE WITH NO CONCLUSION

        CASE WITH FOUR CLOWNS

        CASE WITH ROPES AND RINGS

        CASE FOR SERGEANT BEEF

'Carolus Deene' Novels:

        COLD BLOOD

        AT DEATH'S DOOR

        DEATH OF COLD

        DEAD FOR A DUCAT

        DEAD MAN'S SHOES

        A LOUSE FOR THE HANGMAN

Our Jubilee is Death

by

LEO BRUCE

D

LONDON : PETER DAVIES

FIRST PUBLISHED 1959
PRINTED IN GREAT BRITAIN FOR PETER DAVIES LIMITED
BY RICHARD CLAY AND COMPANY, LIMITED
BUNGAY, SUFFOLK

*Certainly there is no happiness within this circle; ...
the first day of our Jubilee is death.*

SIR THOMAS BROWNE

1

Blessington-on-Sea.
July 22nd.

DEAR CAROLUS,

A slightly unpleasant thing has happened here, and I think the sooner you come down the better for everybody's sake.

I went out for a walk on the sands before breakfast, which one would have thought was an ordinary sort of thing to do at a seaside town. I took Penny and Priss with me because you know how they adore a run, and Penny's been getting rather fat lately, which is most unsightly in a Pekingese. It was last Thursday and really a gorgeous morning with sunlight and a nice breeze.

The tide was going down and I seemed to be the first person to go below the high-water mark, which I always think is thrilling, because you never know what may have been washed up, and I once found a packing-case full of oranges, and although they were no good it was rather exciting.

Well, I was walking along thinking that really one can have quite a good holiday in England in spite of everything people say, when Penny and Priss began to get into a state of wild excitement over something they'd found. It looked from the distance like a rock with a bit of sea-weed on it.

When I got there I saw it was Mrs Bomberger. I mean, her head. Or rather, as I found out later, she was all there, but only her head was stuck out of the sand.

At first I thought (of course I see now I must have been crazy) she was taking a sand-bath or something. She had that awful sort of gracious, condescending smile on her face.

"Good morning, Mrs Bomberger," I said, grabbing Penny and Priss. Then I realized that she was as dead as mutton and that at least one tide had been over her, and her eyes were like oysters.

I suppose I ought to have become hysterical if I was a nice natural girl; but, do you know, I didn't feel a bit like that. I had a little trouble getting the dogs away, but I managed it in the end. I left her exactly where she was and went to phone the police. I only hoped no one short-sighted would come along and trip over her or think she was a ball or anything.

I had the most absurd conversation with somebody at the Police Station, but then, as you know, I'm hopeless at making people understand what I mean, and I don't think the Desk Sergeant was very bright. I'll try to reproduce it for you.

"Oh, this is Fay Deene," I said, and a voice said— "Oo?"

"Well, my name doesn't matter, only it's about Mrs Bomberger . . ."

"Oo?"

"Lillianne Bomberger, you know. The writer of detective novels. You must know her name."

"What about her?"

"Well, she's on the beach. I mean, her head's sticking out of the sand. I'm afraid of someone tripping over it."

"Is this a joke?" asked the voice.

"Well, you may think so," I said, getting rather peeved. "But I shouldn't imagine that she does . . . did. . . . She had no sense of humour, you know. She's dead as a door-nail."

"Now just keep calm, Miss, and let's get this straight . . ."

"I'm perfectly calm," I shouted. "If you want to know, I'm remarkably calm. I'd like to see you as calm as I am if you were having a walk before breakfast and found your-self saying good-morning to a woman who'd been dead for twenty-four hours."

"How do you know she had?"

That was too much.

"I don't know. At least I don't know how *many* hours. But the tide's been over her and her eyes look like oysters that are going off. As a matter of fact it's a wonder she's got any eyes left, with all the shrimps and things."

"Exactly where is the cadaver, Miss?"

"In the sand, if it's anywhere. I mean anywhere with the head because it's only the head that's sticking out. It looks like a production of *Salome*."

"But where in the sand? What part of the beach?"

"Oh, I see. Well, it would be about opposite her house. The Trumbles."

"Ah. And where may you be found, Miss?"

"At the Seaview Hotel. My name's Fay Deene."

"You didn't in any way touch the . . . er . . . lady?"

"Touch her? I always said I wouldn't touch Lillianne Bomberger with a barge-pole when she was alive. I cer-tainly don't want to touch her dead. Not even my dogs wanted that. A sniff was quite enough for them."

"Thank you, Miss. There will be someone round to see you later."

Since then, my dear Carolus, life just hasn't been worth living. She'd been murdered, of course—well, someone was bound to do it sooner or later. The police have done nothing but question everybody, and her two poor nieces will have breakdowns very soon. You can imagine what I'm like when I'm being interrogated. I get in the most frightful muddle and contradict myself, and they begin to look at me.

So, as you'll be Breaking Up in a day or two why not come down and get us all out of the mess? Gracie and Babs Stayer, her nieces, will be delighted. Besides, it's quite amusing, isn't it? that she spent her life creating situations

9

like this and now one has caught up with her. That should appeal to your cold-blooded sense of humour.

Let me know what you're going to do, but, if you can, come and be helpful. We should all be delighted.

Your affectionate cousin,

Fay.

Carolus Deene read this letter over breakfast, then walked across to the school at which he was Senior History Master—the Queen's School, Newminster, a small but proud institution whose headmaster attended the Public Schools Headmasters' Conference every year and so secured its status.

Carolus, a spare, athletic man in his early forties, was more popular among his pupils than in the Common Room. His large private income and casual manner both irritated his colleagues, who acknowledged him to be, however, a clever teacher and a conscientious one. The boys found him somewhat eccentric, but they knew that he had brought fame to the school by a book in which he had applied the principles of modern detection to some of the unsolved crimes of the far past, *Who Killed William Rufus? And Other Mysteries of History*. They also approved of his clothes, his record of a Half Blue for boxing and his Bentley Continental motor-car.

He was considering the letter from his cousin as he entered the school gates. He had read in the newspapers of the mysterious death of Lillianne Bomberger, the enormously successful writer of crime stories, but he had not considered investigating it. He was fond of Fay, whose fiancé had been a fellow-officer of his during the war and was killed at Arnhem. He had made no plans for the coming holidays, but could not bring himself to feel much interest in the fate of Mrs Bomberger. The macabre little picture which emerged from his cousin's letter failed to arouse the curiosity he liked to feel before involving himself in the investigation of a crime.

He might, in fact, have written a refusal to Fay if it had not been for Mr Gorringer, the Headmaster of the Queen's School, a large and ponderous man whose elephantine ears were delicately attuned to every passing rumour. Mr Gorringer appreciated the talents of Carolus as a brilliant teacher, but lived in dread of his bringing notoriety to the school by his passionate interest in crime and the investigations he too readily undertook.

Particularly as school holidays approached Mr Gorringer scanned the popular Press for news of unsolved crimes, unexplained corpses, unarrested murderers, seeing in each a possible attraction for Carolus, and so a potential danger to the school's good name. Two days earlier he had read of the curious situation in which the corpse of Mrs Bomberger had been found and, as he confided to his wife, he trembled.

"I fear, my dear, that it will prove irresistible to Deene. A writer of detective novels up to her neck in the sand of a seaside town! Murdered without a doubt, and partially interred in this extraordinary way! It would seem to have everything that appeals to Deene's perverted curiosity. I fear me the school's name will once again be dragged into headlines. I assure you, I tremble at the prospect."

Carolus, who knew Gorringer and found him, in spite of his pomposity, a rather likeable man, could never resist the temptation to provoke him to take up a manner which in another profession would have brought him a bishopric.

When that morning he saw the headmaster bearing down on him, he guessed what he must expect.

"Ah, Deene," said Mr Gorringer. "So another term draws to its close. Not a day too soon, I feel. Though we can congratulate ourselves on our prowess in the cricket field."

"Going abroad, headmaster?"

"Ostende, Deene. Ostende, as is our custom, with days spent in Bruges, of course. No doubt you will go farther afield?"

"I have not really decided."

"You surely don't think of staying in England, Deene? I should have thought that with your resources you might have sampled the Bahamas, say, or South Africa?"

"No. I don't think I shall go abroad. Some little seaside town, perhaps."

"Let me recommend the Cornish Riviera. A pleasant climate and visitors of an altogether superior stamp, I believe."

"No. I don't think I shall go so far. Some quiet little place on the East coast."

"Ah. But I see you have something in mind. I trust, my dear Deene, that you were not considering anywhere like Blessington-on-Sea?"

"Where's that?"

"Near Laymouth, I believe."

"What's its attraction, headmaster?"

"For me, none, I may say. I can imagine nothing more commonplace and disagreeable after a term's hard work. But I rather feared that recent events in that town might have roused your unfortunate predilection for criminology."

"Why? Has there been a good murder there?"

"A *good* murder? Surely you speak in paradoxes. But you cannot be unaware that a lady novelist of some fame has recently met her death there in unusual circumstances."

"Sounds interesting. Who was she?"

"My dear Deene, the very last thing I wish to do is to arouse in you any interest in something which I consider both repugnant and for a member of my staff highly inadvisable of approach."

"But you do arouse my interest. I was hoping for something of the sort to turn up."

Mr Gorringer stopped in the centre of the quadrangle and faced his Senior History Master.

"Deene, I must make myself clear once and for all. While, of course, I have no authority in matters relating to the private lives of my staff and have never sought to intrude into them, I must say with emphasis that I cannot allow the fair name of the Queen's School, Newminster, to be besmirched by newspaper accounts of your activities. I should certainly never have mentioned this matter had I not reason to fear that you might be already committed."

"I'm not. But who was she?"

"I prefer to say no more. You know my views. I will not have our reputation as a quiet and industrious seat of learning endangered by these criminological antics of yours. I have spoken."

"All right, headmaster. If I do run into a case I'll promise you that my part in it won't become public."

"You do something to allay my fears. But I do indeed wish that you would find other channels for your remarkable abilities. Now I must have a word with our Music Master, whom I see approaching. Ah, Tubley . . ."

Carolus went on to his classroom and faced his most difficult collection of boys, the Junior Sixth. He decided to plunge straight into the last years of Abraham Lincoln.

He found as usual an attentive audience for the first twenty minutes of the period. Lincoln's loss of popularity because of the privations and unnecessary sufferings of the Federal Army in 1864, the saving of his prestige and leadership by Sheridan's victory at Shenandoah, his second term as President and his plans for assisting reconstruction in the Southern States, all seemed to interest at least those in the front two rows, and even the habitual yawners at the back were not noticeably listless.

But when Carolus came to the final scene the attention of the class grew positively fervent.

"An American actor named John Wilkes Booth, twenty-six years old, was responsible for Lincoln's death. He was the son of an English actor who is said to have rivalled Edmund Kean. His elder brother, Edwin Thomas Booth, was the greatest Hamlet of his day and Lincoln's assassin had acted with him. On the night of April 14th, 1865, when Lincoln was watching a play from a box in Ford's Theatre, John Wilkes Booth crept into the box behind him and shot him through the head. He then produced an enormous knife, leapt upon the stage and escaped from the theatre. Twelve days later he was found hidden in a barn and shot."

A studious, harmless-looking boy called Simmons, who was often deputed to draw Carolus from discussion of ancient history to contemporary crime, asked a question.

"Why the knife, sir?"

Carolus was on his guard.

"I do not see that it has much to do with the history of the United States in the nineteenth century, Simmons, and that is what concerns us now."

"But surely, sir, the murder of a President . . ."

"He was shot. Through the head from behind."

"How do we know it was Booth? The box was presumably in darkness. Suppose someone had paid this wretched man to leap about with a knife as soon as he heard a pistol-shot? He was unbalanced, anyway. What proof is there that he committed the murder?"

"History . . ." began Carolus, but he was interrupted by an odiously sophisticated boy called Rupert Priggley.

"Simmons has surely got a point there, sir. It's no more improbable than some of your solutions of modern mysteries."

"I think we will return to the question of Secession."

"Booth was never tried, was he, sir? We don't even know who else may have been in the conspiracy."

"There is no reason to think that anyone was. Booth was a fanatic, if not more. It is an accepted fact that he acted on his own initiative."

"And *you* are talking of 'an accepted fact', sir! I suppose it is an 'accepted fact' that Mrs Bomberger was murdered by one individual and planted in the sand like a cactus?" suggested Rupert Priggley.

"Nothing of the sort," said Carolus warmly, falling headlong into the trap. "Mrs Bomberger was a heavy woman . . ."

"But she used a bath-chair. One man could have wheeled her down there, dead or alive."

"We do not even know what caused her death."

"No, but you soon will, won't you, sir? You can't wait to get down to Blessington-on-Sea. Anyone could see that you're all steamed up and rarin' to go."

"I've no plans at all for these holidays."

"Perhaps you're thinking of joining the headmaster at Ostende, with days in Bruges?"

"Don't be disrespectful, Priggley. After Lincon's death . . ."

"There seems to be a delicious collection of suspects *chez* Lillianne Bomberger. Not the most popular of women, one gathers. And who was Bomberger? Or who is he?"

"I haven't the smallest idea."

"Oh, come on, sir. Don't be naif. We've listened like owls to all that hu-ha about Abolitionists. Give us the dirt now. Who bumped off Lillianne Bomberger?"

"Your guess is as good as mine. I haven't studied the case."

"You think more than one person is involved?"

"I don't know. Now will you all write a brief note on the Emancipation Proclamation? No. We will have silence, please, Priggley. And don't sigh in that offensive way."

Rupert Priggley obediently picked up pen and paper.

"Do you know, sir," he said as he began to write, "you're becoming more like Mr Hollingbourne every day? 'We will have silence, please.' Anyone would think you were a schoolmaster."

2

BEFORE answering his cousin's letter Carolus decided to find out a little more of Lillianne Bomberger than had appeared in the Press, and with this object he called on her publishers, Messrs. Stump and Agincourt, whose offices were discreetly situated in Mount Street. He slightly knew one of the partners, William Agincourt, and asked for him.

He was shown into a waiting-room dominated by a large photograph of a larger woman signed *To my dear Barabbas, Recognizantly, Lillianne Bomberger*. He saw the great pumpkin face and full lips, the monumental hair-do, the seemingly inflated bust and the rapacious eyes of the novelist. She was dressed in something that the late Queen Mary might have worn for her Diamond Jubilee, and afloat in the air behind her, apparently, the photographer had artfully caught the vague shapes and titles of her books.

Mr Agincourt was a stocky, nondescript man, known as the lesser of the two partners in intelligence, personality and capital. He dealt with sales and production, leaving more delicate questions to his famous partner George Stump.

"Morning, Mr Deene," he said when Carolus sat in his Louis Seize office. "Come to offer us a book, I hope? We ought to have had your *Rufus*, and I told George Stump so at the time. Still, I suppose we owe it to you we've got your boss's book."

"What did you say?"

"Oh. Didn't you know? *The Wayward Mortar-board or Thirty Years on the Slopes of Parnassus*, by Hugh Gorringer, Headmaster of the Queen's School, Newminster. Due in the spring. Illustrated. Twenty-five bob."

"Have you read it?"

"Read it? No. I shouldn't think that's possible, but we'll sell it all right."

"It was not what I came to see you about."

"No? Well, what can I do for you? I've got a spare hour."

"What did you know of Lillianne Bomberger?"

"Good heavens, Mr Deene! I said an hour, not a life-time. It would take me from now till Christmas to tell you the half of it. Why? Are you interested in doing the official biography? George Stump wants to find some-one."

"No. I'm afraid not. You'd better get hold of Hector Bolitho or someone who is accustomed to dealing with Royalty. I just want a few facts. Where did she come from?"

"Forest Hill. Small sweet-and-tobacco shop."

"Really. How did she do it?"

"I'll tell you. Sheer hard work and ambition. She never had any looks, any charm, any talent or any money. But she had determination. She won a scholarship to a Gram-mar School as a girl. Started writing before she was twenty. Never published anything, but went on and on. Reckoned to send out so many manuscripts a week whatever hap-pened. It doesn't matter whether you can write or not when you're like that. Sooner or later you get there."

"And Bomberger?"

"That was her big mistake. He was a little, inflammable gasbag of a man who told her he was going to set the Thames on fire, and she believed him. Her name was Lily Cribb before she married, and she'd have done better to keep it. But no, out she came with Lillianne Bomberger, and just at that time she sold a serial to a woman's paper and used the name. She's been stuck with it ever since."

"What happened to Bomberger?"

"He got five years for diamond-smuggling. But that was after she'd been using the name for a year or two, so she couldn't change it. He came out a long time ago, but I don't know whether she ever saw him."

"Who are these nieces who lived with her?"

"They're the daughters of one of her sisters. It was a big family. Decent, respectable people who still live in South East London and wouldn't admit to being tied up with Lillianne Bomberger. But there's a son of one of her brothers whom she set up as a farmer. Somewhere near her home at Blessington-on-Sea."

"That's a fairly imposing sort of house, I take it?"

"Ghastly. George Stump is down there now. It was just outside the little town, the only house in a bay of its own. She bought the land right to the foreshore and would like to have bought that, too. The house was built by one of the tobacco barons, a mock-Gothic affair, not enormously large, but very comfortable. Panelling everywhere. It always seemed to me as though that tobacco man wanted to live inside one of his own cigar-boxes. But it was an easy house to run. She hated having servants. The nieces and the secretary and a char did everything."

"I understand she was a semi-invalid?"

"She posed as one. Had herself pulled about in a bath-chair and all that. I don't think there was much wrong with her health. I think she used hypochondria as a means of dominating the lives of the wretched people round her."

"She doesn't sound very amiable."

"She was a bitch, Mr Deene. The bitch of all time, if you want it straight. An egotist on a scale you can scarcely believe. *Folie de grandeur*, and with it a morbid selfishness and pettiness which were quite terrifying to see. The only surprising thing about her murder is that it did not happen years ago."

"Tell me about her success."

"That was phenomenal, of course. I'll be frank and admit that she has made this firm. Made it. She started with light sentimental novels in the style of Ethel Dell, but got nowhere with them. You have to be sincere for that job. All the successful ones believe in their books as though they were George Eliot. Doesn't matter what tripe it is, it won't get across if they don't believe in it. She didn't. Then she began trying to imitate Mrs Agatha Christie. That didn't work either because Agatha Christie is inimitable. Haven't enough tried? She may have a formula, but gosh! she knows how to work it. Lillianne didn't. But she couldn't be put off. She was forty now, and hadn't had a sniff of success. Then do you know what she did? Combined the two forms of imitation. Wrote a sentimental love-story with wilting heroine and strong, silent men in the Dell manner and popped a murder mystery right in the first chapter. Remember her first? *Blood on the Rose?* We took it, and its success nearly broke us. We hadn't the capital to print what we needed. Fortunately George Stump got some for us and saved the situation. The book sold a hundred thousand at seven-and-six—pre-war, of course. The play ran a year here and nearly two in New York. The film rights brought her a fortune, and it was before Income Tax made such things almost worthless. She never looked back."

"But did she look forward? Did she break new ground?"

"Never, of course. She wrote the same book over and over again to the end. We've got her latest in the office now—*The Flower of Death*. But don't think we've not earned it. We've had her for twenty-three years, and it's been like a prison sentence. She was the most insufferable human being of this century. Or any other, I sometimes think. I wish you had known her."

"I wish that, too. I'm going down to Blessington-on-Sea tomorrow."

"Oh, I see. Going to solve the mystery, are you?"

"A little criminological vacation, I prefer to say. might ask a few questions."

"So far as I'm concerned, whoever did for her was a public benefactor."

"Oh no," said Carolus sharply. "No murderer is that."

Bill Agincourt looked quite serious.

"Suppose someone had succeeded in murdering Hitler?" he challenged.

Carolus smiled.

"I must fall back on words. That would have been political assassination. This was for private, probably selfish, motives. Moreover, you did not mean what you said, I hope. Would you have murdered her?"

"No. Perhaps not. But I could have been tempted to."

"I think you're talking somewhat loosely. But then I'm rather a prig on the subject. I don't like murder anywhere by anyone for any motive at all, Agincourt. It's monstrously presumptuous, for one thing. It's assuming the prerogative of God, if you want a noisy phrase. However, we can agree that Lillianne Bomberger was a woman who provoked the worst instincts in everyone about her. Did *no* one like her?"

"The Secretary, perhaps. Alice Pink. Though even in her devotion there seemed to be a kind of hatred. I don't know. You must see for yourself."

"I know what you mean about the Secretary. It is possible to hate someone so much that it becomes a kind of love. But apart from that had she many acquaintances?"

"Oh yes. She used to appear at literary functions occasionally looking delighted with herself, like a great dairy cow who had beaten the milk-yielding records. She had a few hangers-on. Then down at Blessington-on-Sea she liked to pose as Charity. She headed every subscription list in the town. But friends—not one."

"That certainly suggests a wide field. I'm very grateful to you, Agincourt, for giving me so much information."

"George Stump will tell you more. He's still down at Blessington. He went to try to conciliate Bomberger who was throwing a fit of temperament and threatening to leave us. You know George? He's a character. You'll like him. He expects to be down there another week or two, clearing up. He's an executor, you see."

20

Back in his little house at Newminster, Carolus smoked thoughtfully over a whisky-and-soda, then began to act. He dictated a telegram to his cousin. One of his few extravagances was the sending of unnecessarily long and verbose telegrams, and he seemed to enjoy dictating this one.

Decided to come down and try to save you from probably imminent arrest due to your habits of vagueness and prevarication. Stop. Please obtain authority from heirs for me to investigate. Stop. Book me accommodation but shall look for furnished house for possible further stay. What were you doing at Blessington, anyway? Carolus.

Then Carolus rang for his housekeeper. She was a small, severe, efficient woman who was apt to regard Carolus as a small boy who had to be kept out of temptation's way. She had a particular horror of crime and claimed that her husband shared it.

"Oh, Mrs Stick," began Carolus ingratiatingly, "I was thinking of going down to the seaside for a month or two."

"I'm sure a real holiday would do you good, sir," said Mrs Stick guardedly.

"I thought perhaps I might find a furnished flat or something down there because I hear that seaside places are far from full this year. If I can find one, would you and Stick like to close up here and come down for a time?"

"I'm sure we should be very pleased to, sir. I was only saying to Stick, it's a long time since we've been down to the sea."

"Good. Then I'll do my best to find something."

Suddenly Mrs Stick looked at Carolus more narrowly.

"Where did you say it was, sir?"

"I didn't, Mrs Stick. I haven't quite decided. I thought perhaps . . ." Carolus knew that he was overdoing his casualness . . . "I thought possibly somewhere like Blessington-on-Sea."

Mrs Stick turned red.

"I knew as much," she said. "I don't read the daily

paper for nothing. I told Stick this morning, ten to one you'd start poking about in what didn't concern you with this lady novelist buried alive and that. It'll mean all sorts of people coming to the house, I said, and us not knowing from day to day whether you wouldn't be poisoned. No, sir, neither me nor Stick couldn't possibly see our way to coming down to a place where we might be murdered in our beds any night."

"Come now, Mrs Stick, the murder took place well out of the town, you know. It's a nice little place, and with this lovely summer weather . . ."

"I'm not saying we shouldn't have liked a sniff of sea air, sir, and Stick dearly loves a bit of shrimping, but we can't have ourselves mixed up in murders and that, as well you know. I only wish you would find something nicer to interest yourself in, sir. It seems wrong, all those horrible goings-on, and you risking life and limb to find out who's done it."

"I feel sure you wouldn't be involved, Mrs Stick."

A great indecision seemed to be going on in the small woman's mind.

"Of course, if I could feel sure of that . . . but then there are the people coming to call on you and I not knowing whether they're what you call suspects or not. . . . I'm not denying the sea-water isn't a wonderful thing for Stick's rheumatism, but I should never have a moment's peace wondering whether we weren't going to be knocked up in the middle of the night."

"I think you might chance that, Mrs Stick. You would enjoy the change."

"Well . . . I suppose what is to be is to be. When were you thinking of going, sir?"

"Tomorrow. As soon as I find a place for us all I will wire you."

"Then Stick better start packing at once. Oh, one of the young gentlemen was round this afternoon, sir."

'One of the young gentlemen' meant, from Mrs Stick, one

of Carolus's pupils from the Queen's School, Newminster. She regarded most of them with scarcely less hostility and suspicion than she felt for suspects in her employer's cases.

"Which one?" asked Carolus sharply.

"You might guess which one, sir. That one with the airs and graces as if he was a grown-up man."

"Not Priggley?" asked Carolus desperately.

"That's his name, sir."

"What did he want?"

"Asking this, that and the other question about your movements. I gave him questions. 'What's it to do with you what Mr Deene may choose to do?' I said. 'You go off and mind your lessons.' But he only grinned. 'Don't be stuffy, Mrs Stick,' he said, and before I knew where I was I found myself smiling. He's a cheeky young thing, but he *has* got a sort of way with him. I said to Stick afterwards . . ."

"But what questions was he asking?" demanded Carolus anxiously.

"Oh, whether you were thinking of going to Blessington, and that."

"I hope you didn't tell him?"

"I wasn't to know, was I, sir? It was only Stick reading in the paper that made me think of it."

"But did you tell Priggley that you had thought of it, Mrs Stick?" insisted Carolus severely.

Mrs Stick in turn became more her usual disapproving self.

"You've only yourself to blame, sir, if those who know your ways and what you get up to can guess which way the cat will jump."

"You mean, the abominable Priggley may follow me down to Blessington?"

"No, sir. By what he said he will be there before you. He was leaving this afternoon. In anticipation, he said."

Carolus actually and noisily groaned.

3

FAY DEENE, the cousin who had written to Carolus, was a
woman of thirty-five, a competent actress who had never
been a publicized star, but was rarely out of work. Hers
was a face which made people exclaim, "Oh yes, I've seen
her quite often. What *was* it she was in?" She had been in
so many West End productions and so many English films
that it was difficult not to recognize her but hard to recall
her in any one part.

She had played a secretary, a favourite sister, a friend's
wife, a devoted nurse, a good sort, a beloved niece, a dress-
designer, a lady doctor, a famous hostess and a confidential
barmaid, all with grace and confidence, and her more
outré parts had been those of a games mistress, a poison-pen
specialist and a prostitute.

She had a private income, but its proportions had been
greatly exaggerated in stage circles, where most sums of
money are spoken of as enormous or infinitesmal. She could
afford to refuse the work she did not want, but she could not
afford to be temperamental once she had accepted it.
She was a good-looking woman who dressed a little too
simply to be smart. She had a jolly laugh and, as already
indicated, a vague but voluble way of talking.

"Oh, Carolus," she said when he had found her at her
hotel, "this is splendid. My dear, I'm so tired of practically
being called a murderess, and the Stayer girls are desperate.
Of course you'll clear it up in a moment. Can you imagine,
though, just the head with that look of inane grandeur?
Was she meant to be buried deeper, do you think?"

"Where am I staying?"

"Oh, at the Hydro. It's supposed to be the best, but

24

they're *all* hell. I came down to stay with Bomberger, believe it or not. I was in her last play, and she wanted me in her next one. I spent two nights in the house, then fled. It was like Napoleon at St Helena. A sort of sham Court. Revolting. I came here, and used to go out to Trumbles (that's the name of her house) when she wanted to discuss *The Broken Rosary*, her next play."

"You had no open quarrel with her?"

"Heaps. But who hadn't? You should have *seen* her. She really did bestride her narrow world like a Colossus, and those unhappy people round her peeped about under her huge legs or whatever it was. Only, of course, she was a Colossus of mediocrity."

"Why did they stay with her? Those round her, I mean."

"Partly because they had nowhere else to go, I think, and partly because she mesmerized them like a cobra or whatever you call it. They resented everything, but they never seemed to think of rebellion. It made me rather sick. Even Babs . . ."

"That's the younger niece?"

"Yes, and the brighter one of the two. Even she seemed to have thrown in the sponge. When she first went to live with Lillianne she was a nice cheerful girl from South East London—just what you would think from her name. But the Bomberger had broken her. She'd become sullen and unintelligent, though not quite as much a nervous wreck as her sister Gracie."

"What about the nephew?"

"Ron Cribb. His was the worst case of all, in a way. He's married to a woman called Gloria, a handsome blonde who gave him hell if he ever threatened to escape the Bomberger. Lillianne had bought him his farm, you see, and kept the ownership of it while letting him farm it. She had it all tied up so that she could turn him off at a minute's notice, and of course she took full advantage of that. Rather than keep a car herself she had bought one ostensibly

25

for him, but actually to use him as a chauffeur. I once heard him plead that he simply couldn't take her out next day because he had to attend a farm sale a few miles away. It was at lunch and Lillianne blinked twice, very slowly, keeping her lids down for about two seconds each time, then said, 'Of course, Ron, I know the farm needs attention sometimes, indeed I often wonder that you have so much time to go up to London and so on. What I find difficult to understand is that it should need attention at the *one* time when I feel I might be a little better for a drive. As you are perfectly aware, I no longer look for any pleasure in life but a temporary easement of pain. . . . Nor do I expect the smallest consideration or gratitude from any of you. I have learnt better. But when, *for once*, I give you an opportunity at least to behave with common humanity . . .'

" 'All right, Aunt Lillianne. I'll miss the sale.'

" 'Isn't that rather a grudging and ungracious way to talk? It is not as though I often look for some benefit from the car I purchased. No one could be less exigent than I am. It seems to me that on one of the very rare occasions that I ask you to drive me, you might at least affect some willingness, for the sake of good manners if nothing else.' And so on. In the end the wretched young man had to plead with her to go with him. You see what I mean about a cobra? Or is it a boa-constrictor?"

"I do indeed."

"His wife didn't have to suffer all that, and as a matter of fact Gloria seemed almost to enjoy playing up to the Bomberger. She was not one of the household, and I think Lillianne treated her a little better than the rest, even holding her up as a model to Gracie and Babs. 'It sometimes seems to me that Gloria is the *only* one of you who understands what it is to be in perpetual pain. Perhaps she has a less selfish disposition than my own relatives, or perhaps more imagination. At least she does not exhibit the heartless obsession with her own affairs which my nieces have.' But then she was beastly, they once told me, when

Gloria was going to have her baby. 'I do not expect your generation to realize their responsibilities,' she said, 'but I would have thought you might have *considered* before starting a family at my expense. You must *know* that Ron has nothing whatever of his own and may lose the farm if I am not satisfied with him.' Gloria swallowed that at the time, and little Geoff is two years old now, so she may have forgotten it. She never stood up to Lillianne, but seemed able to live with less friction than the rest, perhaps because she was not so much at Trumbles. She let her husband suffer it all, and if he threatened to kick she gave him worse than he got from Lillianne. My dear, do you know what she was *wearing*? The *lot*. A Hartnell gown with a pile of the awful jewellery she went in for. Incredible, isn't it?"

"No. That's not incredible. Tell me about the Secretary."

"Alice Pink. She's a bit of a mystery. I'm not good at that sort of woman. Secretive and sour and servile. She is supposed to have had the worst time of them all. I've even heard that Lillianne used to hit her. She's a yellowish, scraggy woman with apparently no relative or friend in the world, and she has been with Lillianne for more than ten years. She scarcely spoke when I was there, but rushed about doing housework in a harassed way as though every second she was expecting to hear Lillianne's bell. You could understand that because the blasted thing sounded often enough and Pink would leap like a gazelle for the stairs. Can't think why she stayed. No money or promise of money could have made it worth while. Perhaps she was a little mad."

"How did Lillianne Bomberger treat her in public?"

"Oh, with that awful sort of condescending pseudo-graciousness that she had for everyone except her family. 'Miss Pink, I know you won't mind my mentioning it', sort of thing."

"Mentioning what?"

"Something horribly personal, usually. 'But I fear that

27

my headache will get worse unless you can control that sniffing.' Or, 'Miss Pink, I hate to have to point out that my writing-table—on which, after all, everyone of us has to depend for our existence—is in chaos this morning. Nothing less than chaos. If you could manage to give less time and attention to your own concerns and spare a *little* thought for me it would make things less impossible. Thank you.' And poor Alice Pink would fly about like an agitated ant."

"Who else was there?"

"Graveston, the odd man who wheeled her chair. He, apparently, had no sense of humour at all. A lugubrious character who walked about like someone in a funeral procession. It was hard to know what he thought of her."

"What made him stay?"

"Either she overpaid him or she was blackmailing him. I suppose he, like all of them, had what they call Hopes. She was supposed to be a sick woman, though I believe she would have lived to a hundred if she had not been done in. She had presumably promised them all something. The gardener I can understand because he loved his work, had a cottage of his own and did not get much interference. Then there was Mrs Plum, who came in daily. She was all right because the Bomberger never spoke to her, but said everything through Miss Pink or one of the nieces, and they could tone it down. 'Tell that woman that my head is bursting this morning and the noise she is making is torture to me. I quite realize that you all wish to keep her services while they save you from doing the least little thing about the house, but the point is coming at which I shall be able to endure no more. Listen to that! It's as though you needed a herd of elephant to save you trouble.' Then one of them would appeal to Mrs Plum, who was a good sort and did what she was asked for their sake."

"That was all?"

"There was her doctor. Her line with him was the martyred saint. 'Oh, I know you have other patients to consider, Dr Flitcher. My ailments are not the only ones you treat. But if you could have called yesterday you would have seen, I think, what suffering can mean. I don't complain. I don't expect to be believed. But perhaps now you *are* here you could do something to relieve this agonizing pain in my right shoulder.' That sort of thing."

"You certainly give me a very good idea of Mrs Bomberger, Fay. Anyone else?"

"Do you know George Stump, her publisher?"

"No. I know his partner."

"George is known in the trade as 'Gobbler' Stump, but whether that refers to his appearance or his habits I don't know. Could be either. He made a fortune out of Lillianne —but at what cost! You'll meet him, because he is still down here. He's not a lovable man, but I suppose publishers rarely are. He's greedy and aggressive, but I don't see how he could have murdered her. In fact, that's the difficulty with them all. I can see why they should want to murder Lillianne, I can see how they could have, but I can't somehow believe it of any of them."

"That's always the difficulty, my dear Fay. One never can believe it of anyone."

"They're all people like everyone else, if you know what I mean. They have their little eccentricities; but *murder*! It's just incredible."

"I know. It has a way of being. Now I think I'd better go and find my hotel."

"I'll come with you and see you installed."

They drove along the front. It was not many years since Blessington-on-Sea had been no more than a fishing village with cornfields spreading almost to the churchyard. Now it was a watering-place, not large but, like most towns of its kind, pretentious. There was the Grand Euterpean Concert Hall, the Royal Parade with its monstrous bandstand, the Thespis Repertory Theatre and three cinemas whose plastered concrete took imposing shapes among the shops and houses.

Most garish and showy of all was the Royal Hydro, in which Fay had booked a room for Carolus.

"Well, two rooms, really. I thought you might as well have what they call 'the suite' because I suppose you'll be interviewing people half the time. It is 'sumptuously furnished' and 'commands an unbroken view of the sea'."

"Sounds hell."

"It's the very place from which to investigate the death of Lillianne Bomberger."

The hotel was everything Fay claimed for it. The Sun Lounge was floral and glassy, but there was no sun. The Reading Room was full of deep chairs, but there was nothing to read. The Restaurant was a shimmer of starched cloth and silver, but the food was uneatable. The whole place was luxurious in appearance, but the service was a disgrace.

A girl who looked like a graduate and spoke like a bored and weary waitress received Carolus at the desk.

"Deene?" she said. "Ey'll see. No, we've nothing in that neem."

"But I came here yesterday and booked it," said Fay.

"Who did you speak to?"

"I saw some young female with glasses."

"Oh well, if you saw her, anything ken have heppened Did she give you a number?"

"No. She said 'the suite'."

"Oh, the suite. Whey didn't you say so? Thet's rate. The suite's booked in the neem of Deene. I thought you meant an ordinary room."

She turned over pages while Carolus waited for his key.

"It surprises me, reelly, that she remembered to write it down," went on the young woman in a fatigued voice. "She never does. Ey'll see if Ey ken get someone to take your beggage, only they're all Off now."

She began to press bell-buttons.

"Ey was afreed not," she said, when no one appeared. "It's their tea-tame. They're supposed to leave someone

30

On, but there you are. Ey'll send it up presently if you lake."

Carolus and Fay made for the lift.

"Weet a minute," called the young woman. "Here's Fred." She indicated a ginger-headed man with a grim, unsmiling face. "Oh, Fred, teek this gent's begs up, will you? The suite, et ees."

Fred seemed to think the matter over, then laboriously picked up some of Carolus's luggage.

"I should think Lillianne Bomberger would have loved this place," said Carolus to Fay.

The young woman overheard him.

"Es a metter of fect she deed," she admitted. "She keem here quate often. She was here hevving tea on her lest efternoon, as a metter of fect."

"Really? Alone?"

"No. With the young man who used to drave her."

"You say, to tea?"

"Yase. We do a fave-shilling tea in the Spanish Patio every day. Phil Phillips and his Phillipines. It's very popular. Mrs Bomberger frequently keem."

"My God!" said Carolus.

"Ey noticed her thet lest efternoon," went on the young woman. "Ey thought she looked very tired and put out about something. But Ey may have been misteeken. Here's your key."

"Thank you."

But another shock awaited Carolus. When he eventually discovered 'the suite'—Fred not having bothered to wait to show it him—he found the door of the sitting-room open. He went in to see, stretched in the deepest arm-chair with a cigarette and a book, the neatly-dressed figure of Rupert Priggley. The boy rose to his feet.

"Don't say it, sir," he commanded.

"What?" asked Carolus, taken off his guard.

"Don't say 'What are you doing here, Priggley?' Yes, I see you were just going to. I'm waiting for you, of course."

31

"Why?"

"Really, you do make one obvious, sir. To begin working on the Bomberger case, naturally. Or have you come here for the 'sumptuous furniture' and 'unbroken view of the sea'?"

"I take it you're with your parents?"

"Parents? You know Mummy's having a brand-new divorce. Far the most exciting yet, she says. Daddy's still with that dreary model of his. He's a monogamous type, really. So I've been told to take myself off on the motor-bike to a good hotel by the sea somewhere. How *could* there be a better one than this, in the circumstances? Aren't you going to introduce me?"

Carolus did so.

"I saw you in *The Flying Horse*," said Rupert. "I thought you were terrific. I never knew you were Carolus's cousin."

"So there can be something you don't know?" asked Carolus, but realized that it would do little to repress Priggley.

4

BEFORE seeing anyone connected with the case Carolus obtained and studied a full account of the inquest. From this he learnt a number of interesting and one or two rather startling facts.

The medical evidence had caused something of a sensation. It appeared that Lillianne Bomberger had taken, shortly before her immersion, a sufficient number of sleeping-pills to cause her death, and that although the tide had gone over her the evidence of this remained. Death was believed to have occurred at approximately two to three o'clock in the morning, and low tide had been at two. She had probably been buried in the sand between three and four o'clock, as the tide was coming in, and Fay Deene had discovered her at half-past eight next morning. She was certainly dead before being buried in the sand.

She was dressed, as Fay said, in an elaborate gown which she had not worn during the previous evening. Some jewellery was on her, but none that was kept in the private safe in her bedroom.

The members of her household were broadly in agreement in their evidence. Mrs Bomberger had been in a good mood at dinner that night. She had not drunk more than usual with the meal, but after it had swallowed two glasses of a sweet South African wine, which she very much liked. There had been a game of bridge. She went to bed early— shortly before ten, said some; soon after, said others—and no one had seen her again.

The sleeping-pills had been prescribed for her by Dr Flitcher. Babs Stayer, who usually went up with her aunt when the latter went to bed, explained that Mrs Bomberger was inclined to be secretive about these pills, though she had allowed Babs to have the prescription made up. Babs explained that this was the second box of them and that the earlier one Mrs Bomberger had finished over a long period, never taking them unless she found it necessary. The present box she had put in the cupboard beside her bed and it had not been opened till that night. In the morning six of the pills were missing. Babs agreed that her aunt knew that she should take no more than one at a time. Dr Flitcher explained that three would be dangerous and six, to a woman of Mrs Bomberger's plethoric constitution, almost certainly fatal.

Asked whether it was possible that Mrs Bomberger could have dressed herself and walked to the sands alone, the family agreed that while nothing about her made this absolutely impossible it was so unlikely as almost to be ruled out. It was true that she was lazy and selfish and liked to be driven about in the car or wheeled in the bath-chair, but she was not, in fact, incapable of walking, and as for dressing herself, she did that every day, disliking the assistance of anyone. But it was incredible to them all that she should actually have gone down to the beach in the small hours unaided.

Her absence from the house had not been discovered when the police brought the news of the finding of her body. It was her strict rule that no one should disturb her till she rang, and this was sometimes as late as eleven o'clock. When, however, the police came to the house the room was entered and it was found that the bed appeared to have been slept in, for some time at least.

A rather odd fact which was revealed was that Ron Cribb and his wife were staying in the house that night by Mrs Bomberger's special request. It appeared that on certain occasions she had attacks of nervousness and insisted that there should be a man in the house. Graveston slept in a room beyond the kitchen which had been a housekeeper's sitting-room when a large staff was kept, but this did not satisfy Mrs Bomberger. She would ring up the unfortunate Ron Cribb and Gloria and they would have to leave their baby son Geoffrey with the wife of the farm foreman and come over to Trumbles. This had happened on that Wednesday.

So that, in addition to the dead woman, in the house that night were Ron and Gloria Cribb, Gracie and Babs Stayer, Alice Pink and Graveston. None of them heard anything unusual in the night. None of them, according to their evidence, noticed or guessed or suspected anything amiss until the police arrived with the news of finding Mrs Bomberger's body.

The verdict was an open one, and the Press had rather laboured the irony of this, a creator of murder mysteries whose own death was one.

Carolus digested this information, then, eluding Priggley, called for Fay and asked her to accompany him in a walk along the sands.

"I want to see more or less where you found her," he explained.

It was a warm early evening, and the beach of the town, though not crowded, was well sprinkled with holiday-makers. A cliff rose to the north of this beach, and they rounded this to come into a small separate bay. There were also plenty of people here. One group of trees which seemed to be protecting a house was visible from this beach, but no building was in sight.

"You see? That's Trumbles, her house, and she owns most of the land down to the beach, but not of course the foreshore. So far the town's development schemes have passed her by, but sooner or later all this bay will be taken in to Blessington-on-Sea, I should think. Meanwhile, she can prevent any building here, even of a kiosk or café, so that this beach is used by parties who mean to picnic on the sands more than anything."

"And at night it would be deserted?"

"Oh quite, I should think. I told you, when I came along

35

here that morning, it was half-past eight and I was the first person to tread the sand since the tide went down. The only sound I remember was the seagulls. They screamed away like mad. You might almost have thought they knew what had happened."

"You saw no one?"

"Not a soul. I hurried back to the parade and rushed for a telephone booth. I passed no one in Trumbles Bay, but on the town beach the holiday-makers were beginning to appear."

They were almost midway between the two cliffs which marked off Trumbles Bay like boundary posts.

"It's easy to get up to the house from here?" asked Carolus.

"Oh quite. Nothing to stop you so long as you've a key of the lower gate, and everyone had that."

"When you stayed there I suppose you came down to swim from there?"

"Yes."

"How long did it take to reach the water from the front door?"

"It took *me* the hell of a long time because I loathe cold water. But the distance isn't more than half a mile."

"Now, where was the body?"

"My dear Carolus, I didn't raise a concrete pillar on the spot. I can't tell you to within a yard. But I should say somewhere round about here."

"Which way was the head facing?"

"Inland. She might have been looking at the house."

"There was nothing near it? That you noticed, anyway?"

"Nothing at all. Just the head out of the sand. The sand was perfectly smooth except where the dogs had disturbed it."

Carolus remained there for a few minutes, then started walking slowly in the direction of the house.

"I see there's a stretch of sand which remains above high-water mark."

"Yes."

"You did not cross it that morning?"

"No. I came round the headland and went back the same way. I did not come up to the house. But in any case I wouldn't have seen anything, if you're thinking of tracks. That dry sand is trodden all day."

"Yes. I wasn't thinking of that. But why didn't you go up to the house when you found the Bomberger? It was your nearest telephone."

"Do you know, Carolus, I've never quite known the answer to that one. Why didn't I? It was a bit of a shock finding her head there and not being sure whether there was any *body* to it or not, as it were. I mean you know I'm a fairly unruffled type, but *really*, before breakfast, Bomberger's face grinning up at you . . . well, I was shaken. So I suppose I acted on instinct. I hated that house and everything in it. I just rushed back the way I came. Besides, I may have had some intuition about the people there. Either that they knew nothing about Mrs. Bomberger's death or that they knew too much. I only know that blindly and instinctively I avoided them and phoned the police from a booth on the promenade."

"Quite understandable. Have you seen any of the household since?"

"Oh yes. Quite a lot."

"What's your impression?"

"Well, naturally they're worried and upset. One expects that. But somehow I think it goes farther than that. If you want me to say what I think, it's that they're frightened. Scared stiff."

"Really? Of what?"

"I don't know. They all behave as though they were listening for the ticking of a time-bomb."

"One would have thought they'd be showing signs of relief. Considering what she was, I mean."

"Perhaps that will come later. Just now they're terrified of something. I feel sure of it. Gracie's perhaps the worst. And the police found out about some poison she bought."

"How do you mean?"

"Oh, quite harmless. I don't know whether it was weed-killer or rat-poison, but there was enough of it to kill half a dozen people. Only Gracie had never opened the packet or the tin or whatever it was."

"Then why was she worried about it?"

"I don't know. She was in a fearful tizzy. One way or another, they don't seem able to appreciate their luck yet."

"Are they so lucky? What about the will?"

"From their point of view it's not as good as it might be because she leaves a thumping big sum to found a Literary Award. There's quite a large annuity in perpetuity for The Lillianne Bomberger Prize for the Best Detective Novel of the Year. It is to be chosen by a committee consisting of the Commissioner of Metropolitan Police, the Vice Chancellor of Oxford University, the President of the PEN Club, the Chairman of the Publishers' Association and the Editor of *The Times Literary Supplement*. It takes quite a bite out of her capital, but it leaves those round her a few thousand each, with larger allotments to the relatives, Gracie and Babs Stayer and Ron Cribb. There is nothing for Ron's little son and nothing for any other member of her family. Pink and Graveston are well looked after, and the doctor and gardener get quite handsome sums. There is something for her husband, if he still exists."

"Do you think he does?"

"Yes. I'm almost sure. But I should imagine that Pink knows for certain."

They could see the house, surrounded by trees and shrubs and looking rather gloomy now that the sun was down. Carolus stood watching for a time, but nobody was in sight. The ugly Gothic structure had open windows, but otherwise might have been uninhabited.

"Can we go back over the cliff?" asked Carolus.

38

"Yes. There's a footpath."

They climbed steadily upwards from the bay, and when Carolus reached the top he said, "I can't think why Lillianne's murderer wanted anything more elaborate than this. She had her bath-chair. A small push as he left her and an easy 'accident' could have been staged."

"It would have to be after dark," said Fay. "There's the coastguard station along there with windows commanding most of the cliff. Besides, this footpath is used a lot, as you see."

"Was she ever wheeled up here?"

"Yes, oddly enough, lately she insisted on it, I think because Graveston could scarcely pull her up the hill. He would suggest other ways to go, but she would say, 'No, Graveston, I'm very well aware that you wish to avoid any little extra trouble and that the perfectly idle life you have here makes even the smallest effort unwelcome to you. But though I have learnt to sacrifice myself to the whims of you all, there are things on which I must insist if I am to live any longer. One of them is fresh upland air such as we found at the cliff-top. We will take that route. Thank you.' Then Graveston would puff and sweat up this hill path."

They could see Blessington-on-Sea stretched out in a crescent beneath them, with the Royal Hydro Hotel the most conspicuous building of all.

"I simply can't stay at that place," Carolus confided. "I never know whether I'm in the Spanish Patio or the Viennese Lounge. I must find a flat, or something, even if it's only for a fortnight."

They bought the *Blessington-on-Sea Advertiser* and began to look through the Accommodation to Let column without much encouragement. But at the foot was a small note *Wee Hoosie, Sandringham Terrace, 2 sit 2/3 bed, mod cons, Reliance geyser, let furn immed. Apply premises.*

"No, Carolus," said Fay. "There is a limit. Even to escape the Royal Hydro. The Sticks wouldn't stand for it."

"I suppose not," said Carolus, and they parted.

But when he reached the Royal Hydro, the young woman whom he had seen on arrival was in wait for him.

"Oh, Mr Deene," she said, "Ey'd not the slatest ideea you were the detective. Ey faind it quate interesting. Ey don't ectually read many novels because Ey haven't the tame, but Ey know your neem well."

Carolus stared blankly at her as though waiting to know where this would lead.

"It must be quate a nace lafe, being a detective. No wonder your were interested en what Ey was eble to tell you ebout Mrs Bomberger. Oh, end Ey've telephoned to a gentleman friend of mane who is on the *Blessington Edvertiser*, and he's coming to call on you this efternoon. Ey thought it would be nace for you to have the publicity and so on."

Carolus fled to his car and drove to Sandringham Terrace. He found Wee Hoosie, a semi-detached brick villa, and rang the bell. This brought a head from the door in the other half of the semi-detachment.

"She's away," said a woman without preliminaries. "I'm looking after it. If you want it it's eight pounds a week with everything in except light where there's a metre and coal which you get by the sack from Simmonses. She's got linen and that and the place is spotless, because I do it myself and could go on obliging if anyone wanted though not in the evening."

"When could I move in?"

"Well, there's nothing to stop you once you pay a week in advance, which you can do to me, because she didn't want agents and that mixed up with it and keeping half it for themselves. I mean you could move in today if you wished, only you better have a look to see if it suits."

Carolus took a hurried and somewhat disturbing glance at a front room having a plush-covered dining-table, a cottage piano with brass candle-holders, six black horsehair chairs, billowing lace curtains on wooden rings and poles, and a collection of large framed photographs chiefly of weddings. He hastily wondered how he would be able to enter himself into this crowded arena, but thought that even if it was by crawling on all fours under the table it was better than the Royal Hydro.

He pulled out eight pound notes and handed them to the woman, who said she would give him the receipt later.

"Of course she has got rather a lot of stuff," she admitted, "and the bedrooms are the same. It's through her having come into all her sister's things just after their mum died who had a much bigger house on Victoria Hill. Still, you'll find your way about, I expect. Mind that hat-stand! I've caught myself a nasty knock on there before now, and what she wants with this china umbrella thing I can't think, but there you are, she won't part with anything."

Carolus drove, too fast he feared, to the Royal Hydro and packed his bags. Then he stopped at a post office and sent off a wire to his housekeeper and returned to Wee Hoosie. It was only then he realized that he had missed his lunch.

5

NEXT day he started direct investigation by paying a call on Ron Cribb.

He found Beddoes Farm about five miles inland, an isolated group of buildings on the open Suffolk countryside. There was a rough road up to the house, which stood a little apart from the farm and faced towards the sea. It was a typical small farm-house of the eighteenth century with a modest portico and one long window on each side of it.

The door was opened by Gloria Cribb, and had he only heard her name and not remembered Fay's description of her as a 'handsome blonde' he would have known who she was.

"Oh *yes*," she said, "Fay told us about you. Come in."

She sat opposite to Carolus, and although her manner was not altogether easy she spoke in a pleasant, good-humoured voice.

"I may as well confess that I personally was against having you in on this. I'm sure the police will clear it up, and in any case it doesn't seem all that important to know who killed Lillianne Bomberger, even if anyone did. But I was overruled. That doesn't mean I shall be awkward about it. I'll answer any questions you like."

"You said something rather interesting then, Mrs Cribb. 'Even if anyone' killed Mrs Bomberger. Do you think it might have been suicide?"

"Could be. Why not?"

"She couldn't very well have buried herself in the sand, could she?"

"No. I don't say that. But that's not what killed her. I mean it's possible she killed herself. Or it could have been an accident. I can't see that it was certainly murder."

Carolus had the impression that Gloria was now talking for the sake of it. She seemed to have become restless and uncomfortable.

"But surely that would be terribly out of character, wouldn't it? To commit suicide, as far as I understand it, would be to oblige almost everyone—the last thing she would wish to do."

Gloria smiled nervously.

"I suppose so. Unless she had some reason that we don't know about. But you talk as though we all wished her dead. I don't think it went as far as that. She was intolerable in many ways, and I don't think there was anyone really fond of her, but I shouldn't like to say more than that."

"Tell me about that last day."

"So far as I was concerned nothing happened till about six o'clock, when I heard Ron on the phone and guessed what it was."

"What was he saying?"

"He was trying to get us out of going over to Trumbles. This was always happening. She would take it into her head that she would like to play Bridge in the evening and phone to ask us to dinner. We would accept and then, just before the conversation finished, she would say she wanted us to stay the night. She was nervous and wanted a man in the house. That evening Ron was really quite firm. He said that Mrs Beale, our foreman's wife who used to look after my small son, was ill and it was impossible."

"Was she ill?"

"She wasn't very well. But that was nothing to Lillianne. 'Really, Ronald, if you are so irresponsible as to start a family when you have no means of supporting it . . .' That sort of thing. In the end, of course, we gave in.

"When we arrived there, she was all smiles. She had got her own way, you see. That always tickled her. We had dinner and the usual four at Bridge, Ron and I against Lillianne and Babs. Lillianne played quite well—she was the best Bridge player of us in any case. And oddly enough she behaved herself reasonably well over the game and never held post-mortems. That evening she won a little, and went off to bed at something shortly before ten. Then a phone-call came through."

"It's the first I've heard of that."

"It was soon after ten. Alice Pink answered it. A man's voice asked for Mrs Bomberger. Alice said, 'Who's speaking?' and the voice said, 'Tell her Mr Green wants to speak to her. She'll understand.' Rather an odd thing to say, we thought."

"Rather. Yes."

"Alice got through to Lillianne. The house has extensions everywhere. She told Lillianne what the man had said, and Lillianne shouted 'What?' as though she wouldn't believe it. Then she said, 'Put him through', which Alice did."

"No one listened to the conversation?"

"No. You can tell when the receiver's off the hook. Alice wouldn't dare. But it went on for some minutes."

"None of you had any idea who Mr Green might be?"

"We discussed it, of course. We came to the conclusion that the one thing we knew about him was that he wasn't Mr Green. Nobody would give a name and say, 'She'll understand', if that was his own name. But we'd no idea who it was. She didn't often get telephone calls because she let it be known that they disturbed her."

"Did you hear or see any more of her that night?"

"Not really. Apparently she phoned down to Alice Pink and told her to get us all off to bed as soon as she could. It disturbed her to know we were sitting downstairs and perhaps discussing her. Besides, one of her meannesses was electricity. We broke up before eleven."

"That's all? Nothing during the night?"

"Nothing."

"Thank you, Mrs Cribb. I wonder if I can see your husband?"

"Ron's working on the car. You'll find him in the

garage just across the yard. If he gave as much time to the farm as he does to his car . . ."

"An enthusiast? I'm told I'm just as bad."

"He likes messing about. I say, he makes trouble just to put it right. And he won't take anything to the garage. He's really obstinate about that. Lately, for instance, his battery's been down, and rather than have it charged up he has been using the starting-handle every time."

Carolus smiled.

"That is carrying things rather far," he admitted.

"Anyway, you'll find him across there. That middle shed. Perhaps you'll bring him over for a drink when you've asked what you want?"

"Thank you very much."

When Carolus stood in the entrance to the garage he could see no one, but sounds were coming from under the car. Lying beside it was a new brake-cable.

"Mr Cribb," he said.

The sounds stopped. There was a long pause. Then Ron Cribb emerged looking, Carolus decided, nothing short of terrified. No ordinary summons to a man in a normal condition of mind could have produced those staring eyes in a drawn face, that look of amazement and horror.

"Who . . . who are you?" he asked, never taking his eyes from Carolus.

"My name's Deene. Your wife said I should find you here. Putting in a new brake-cable?"

Carolus was trying to be calming and chatty.

At first he thought that Ron Cribb was going to seize the brake-cable from where it lay. He looked at it then back to Carolus.

"What . . . what . . ." he mouthed.

"I understood from my cousin Fay that you didn't mind my coming down and asking a few questions about Mrs Bomberger's death. I'm sorry if I startled you."

"Startled? No, no. I didn't hear you coming, that's all. I was working."

45

"Hand-brakes are a bore. Cable broken?"

"No. Worn. Let's go over to the house."

"I hear you're like me—you loathe having other people to do your repairs. I've never put in a new brake-cable, though. Tricky?"

"No. Easy enough. I've had enough of it now, though. Been working for more than an hour."

"I hear your battery's down."

"Who told you that?" flashed Ron Cribb angrily. "What business? . . . I'm taking it in today."

"Where do you go for repairs when you're forced to? I shall probably need something while I'm here."

"Lindon's. They're the best. Let's go over to the house."

Carolus seemed to turn away unwillingly. When they reached the house Gloria had evidently been upstairs to 'tidy herself' and looked rather splendid with her brilliant fair hair and good full figure. She at once offered them drinks. Carolus noticed when Ron was pouring himself a stiff whisky that his hand was trembling.

They chatted in a desultory way about Lillianne Bomberger and her last evening, but Carolus was careful to ask no leading questions and show no great curiosity. Presently the conversation turned to his own Bentley Continental, and Ron showed an intelligent interest.

"Would you both care to see how you like it?" asked Carolus. "Why not come for a little run and have lunch with me in Norwich? I'm told that there's one decent restaurant."

Gloria was pleased, but Ron, who was a little surly-looking at the best of times, said slowly, "I want to finish the job I'm doing."

"You can do that when we come back," said Gloria peremptorily, and her husband could not very well refuse to go.

Carolus drove them northward, skirted Yarmouth, and was able to open up on the main Yarmouth-to-Norwich road. They spoke little, luxuriating in the big car's smooth performance at speed.

In Norwich he pulled up at a restaurant called the Brass Owl, and they went into a large, comfortable room. Settling his guests at a table, he excused himself and made for the telephone.

Luckily Rupert Priggley was in the dining-room of the Royal Hydro.

"You didn't tell me you were leaving this fearful hotel," reproached Rupert.

"No. I hoped to shake you off. But I don't know whether you most resemble a burr or a leech."

"A lure or a bitch? Hard words, aren't they, sir? And now I suppose you want me to be useful."

"Yes. Got a pen? Go out at once to Beddoes Farm, about five miles inland from Trumbles Bay. I've got the farmer and his wife here to lunch in Norwich, so you won't see them. In the yard behind the house is a garage, and in that a Morvin four-seater. Beside it on the floor is a new brake-cable. Got all that?"

"Yes. Exactly."

"I want you to make a careful examination of the old brake-cable. Is it worn out? Was it ordinary wear and tear? And so on. If anyone sees you there you've come by Mr Cribb's orders to take the battery to be recharged. Get away as soon as you can, but not until you've made a thorough examination."

"Shall be done. Where shall I see you?"

"At the house I've taken furnished."

"Address?"

"Wee Hoosie . . ."

"I beg your pardon?"

"You heard perfectly well. Wee Hoosie, Sandringham Terrace. You can wait about there till I get back. That will be in a couple of hours."

Carolus returned to his guests to find Ron more sullen than before. A good meal failed to cheer him, and he expressed anxiety to return to his farm.

"So much to do," he muttered fretfully.

47

Carolus did not think it necessary to delay their return much longer, for it was past three before he eventually dropped the couple at their front door and drove into Blessington.

Priggley was astride his motor-cycle at the gate of Carolus's temporary home.

"The Sticks arrived, took one look at Wee Hoosie and fled," said Rupert.

"You don't mean they've gone back to Newminster?"

"It would be no more than you deserved if they had. 'Wee Hoosie'! It makes me sick to my stomach. But they've only gone for a walk. Their luggage is in the coal-shed."

"Come in," said Carolus, opening the front door and revealing the hat-stand and umbrella-pot.

"I think I would rather not, if you don't mind, sir. I'm no archaeologist, and I've always had rather a thing about tombs."

"Inside!" snapped Carolus, and Priggley opened the door of the front room. He quickly closed it again.

"I feel one owes some respect to the dead," he said unctuously.

"What dead?"

"All dead. Everywhere. It smells of them."

"Bit musty, perhaps. Open a window."

"Did you say musty, sir? Yes, I thought you did. I don't argue over words. But don't talk in that frivolous way of opening windows. Even if there was room for me to reach them, they're obviously not made to be opened till all the other tombs give up their dead."

When Carolus had squeezed his way across and pulled aside the lace curtains he found that Priggley was right.

"And what do you suppose these are?" asked the odious boy, indicating the wedding groups.

"Family photographs," suggested Carolus.

"You relieve me. I thought they were illustrations for the case-histories of one of our bolder psychiatrists."

"Suppose you tell me what you have to report?"

"You'll find it disappointing. The old cable had been eaten away by acid from the battery which was just above it. Perfectly natural."

"Think so?"

"Why not?"

"You may be right. It's rather a coincidence that the battery was flat and Cribb wouldn't take it in to be recharged."

"Anyway, the Bomberger was poisoned and died of an overdose of sleeping-pills and was found buried in the sand, so what's a brake-cable to do with it?"

"I like collecting scraps of information. Did anyone see you out there?"

"Not that I know of. I left everything as I found it. So you're not disppointed in my information?"

"Dear me, no."

At that moment there was knocking at the back door and Rupert admitted the Sticks. Mrs Stick hastily and fearfully glanced round the kitchen, which held among other miscellaneous effects a walnut Victorian couch, a wicker arm-chair, a grandfather clock and a quantity of fire-irons which appeared from their size and variety to be intended to stoke the furnace of an iron-smelting works. A kitchen range, a vast coal-scuttle and stacks of china which overflowed an enormous dresser left her just room to pass sideways across the room. In awful silence she viewed the entrance passage and mounted the stairs. The three males below heard her open each door in turn and descend again.

"Well, Mrs Stick?" said Carolus heartily.

"I beg your pardon, sir, but did you see over the rooms before taking the house?" she asked.

"Not all of them, Mrs. Stick. Why?"

"It's not for me to say, sir. Only I never thought that Stick and me would have to get into bed by hopping over a hip-bath and vaulting a clothes-horse. And I wouldn't have supposed you want three commodes and a what-not in your room."

"It's through her having come into her sister's things just after their mum . . . mother died," explained Carolus. "She won't part with anything."

Mrs Stick sniffed.

"It's clean, isn't it?" asked Carolus.

"It's clean, yes, sir. But how's it going to be kept clean, that's what I want to know? If I can't get into the rooms, how am I going to dust them? As for cooking anything— well, there's nowhere to put any food if you was to buy it, and whoever did the beds must have been a contortionist made of india-rubber, which Stick and me are not. Where your clothes are going goodness only knows, but I shouldn't be able to unpack them even if we found room for a shirt or two. I've already nearly tripped over a hassock and a slop-pail, and upstairs there's texts on all the walls and wash-stands and corner-brackets and dressing-tables wherever you turn."

A relief was provided by the arrival of his next-door neighbour with Carolus's receipt.

"I've got an empty bedroom," she volunteered, "where you could put some of it if you can't manage. I'm sure she wouldn't mind that. It would give you room to turn round, wouldn't it?"

They set to work.

6

Carolus felt that he could no longer postpone a visit to the dead woman's home, and that evening decided to go with his cousin to Trumbles. He felt that, introduced by Fay, he would be less formidable and less annoying to the three women, who, he gathered, appeared to be near distraction after the horror of the murder itself, the inquest and the searching enquiries of the police.

He started on the road he had taken that morning when on his way to Beddoes Farm, but on Fay's instructions turned left by a narrow lane which led only to the house. It looked much as Agincourt had said, modern Gothic and ugly.

As they drew near they met an individual walking towards them, and Carolus slowed down.

"Who's this?" he asked Fay.

"Never seen him before."

"Not the odd man or the gardener?"

"No."

The question was scarcely necessary, for the man looked raffish and seedy, not in the least like someone who worked for steady wages. Carolus thought there was something suggesting the gypsy about him, yet that was not quite what he appeared. Fairground? Just possibly. He was a tallish man with a squint and a mirthless grin with which he replied to Carolus's stare, showing a number of gold teeth.

The front door was opened by Alice Pink, to whom Fay introduced Carolus. They went into a large panelled room full of ill-arranged flowers and met Gracie and Babs Stayer. But before taking note of his surroundings Carolus asked about the man in the lane.

"Just *now*?" said Gracie Stayer. "There has been no one here this afternoon."

"No one," repeated Alice Pink solemnly.

"But he must have been coming from the house," said Fay, and described the man they had seen.

"What an extraordinary thing!" exclaimed Babs, who, like the other two, seemed very disturbed by these questions. "Not a soul has been here, I assure you."

"Could he have been to see someone else in the house?"

"There is no one else. Graveston has gone to Laymouth and the gardener left two hours or more ago. Besides, we should have heard." Gracie Stayer sounded genuinely perplexed and nervous. "It is yet another mystery connected with this ghastly affair."

Carolus at once confirmed in his mind an anomalous aspect of the whole case. Everyone agreed that Lillianne Bomberger was an odious woman, everyone thought she should have been murdered years ago, everyone knew that those round her had been relieved by her death of an intolerable strain, yet neither in these three women nor in the couple he had seen this morning was there any suggestion of relief; on the contrary, they looked ill with worry and anxiety.

Gracie Stayer was tall and dark and gave the impression of being prematurely old. Sad, anxious eyes looked out from a face which, though not actually lined, was drawn and tired. She was the kind of young woman who is called intense.

Suddenly she said in a voice which suggested hardly repressed hysteria, "I should like to speak to you, Mr Deene. Alone." Then, turning to the others as though to explain, she said, "Well, I *must* have advice from someone who understands these things."

Fay tactfully rose, and Babs Stayer and Alice Pink accompanied her from the room.

"I don't know what to do," said Gracie. "I don't know *what* to do. The police keep questioning me."

"Perhaps they think you haven't told them the truth, Miss Stayer."

"But I have. It's about the poison, chiefly. You see, I bought some arsenic weed-killer."

"What was that for?"

Gracie Stayer had no sense of fatuity when she replied, "For killing weeds."

"Yes. But I meant what particular weeds?"

"Oh, in the drive," said Gracie eagerly. "There were so many weeds in the drive. Aunt Lillianne hated to see it."

"Did she tell you to get the weed-killer?"

"No. She didn't actually tell me."

"You have a gardener, haven't you?"

"Primmley, yes."

"Why didn't you tell him to deal with the weeds, Miss Stayer?"

This question seemed particularly to upset Gracie Stayer. She pulled at her handkerchief, and Carolus wondered if she was going to start crying.

"You're as bad as the police," she said resentfully.

"I only want to arrive at the truth. I can't be of much use to anyone till I know the truth."

"But on this I can't answer you. I don't *know* why I didn't tell Primmley. It was an impulse, I suppose. I thought of the weeds when I was in Cupperly's—the chemists—and asked them if they had a good weed-killer. They showed me this and I bought it. That was all."

"You see, Miss Stayer, perhaps the police think it rather odd that a member of the household who is not usually concerned with the garden should suddenly, without consulting the gardener, purchase weed-killer."

"Yes, but the tin was never opened. They could see that. The seal wasn't broken. Yet they have questioned me again and again."

"Interrogation is terribly trying, I know."

"Besides, Aunt Lillianne died of an overdose of sleeping-

53

pills, didn't she? They know that. Why do they have to go on about a weed-killer?"

"I honestly don't know. But the police have a way of reaching the truth in the end."

This did not seem to do much to console Gracie Stayer.

"Would you mind telling me what you were wearing on the night of your aunt's death?"

Gracie Stayer, who had intended to ask Carolus for advice and now found herself narrowly questioned, looked rather baffled.

"I'm just trying to remember," she said, but one could almost hear her saying to herself, 'Why is he asking me this?' "I remember. I had on a black frock—almost new."

"What shoes?"

"Really! Have you found some footprints or something?"

"It would help me if you could tell me that."

"I think it was a black velvet pair."

"Could you be sure?"

'Why is he asking me? Why is he asking me?' said Gracie's tortured eyes.

"Yes, I'm sure it was."

"Were they nearly new, too?"

"Yes, yes."

"Could I see them?"

"Why? Why do you want to see them? No, you can't. It's absurd. I thought you were going to help us, not be fifty times worse than the police. No, you can't see them."

"If you want to get at the truth, Miss Stayer, I will help you. If you have something to conceal, I shall be very far from helpful."

"I *haven't* anything to conceal. Of course I haven't."

"Then would you please show me those black velvet shoes?"

"I can't. I haven't got them. They were uncomfortable."

"What did you do with them?"

"Oh, I can't remember now. Gave them to Mrs Plum."

Carolus pretended to make a note, which seemed to agitate Gracie further.

"No. I'm not sure what I did. Threw them away, I think. Put them in the dustbin. That was it."

"Wouldn't it be better to tell me the truth about this, Miss Stayer?"

"I'm telling you all I remember."

"It is just as you wish, of course."

"But I *am* telling you all I remember."

"What time did you go up to your bedroom that evening?"

"About eleven, I think."

"Did you go straight to bed?"

"Yes."

"Read in bed?"

"Sometimes. Not that night."

Gracie was calmer.

"No one came to your room during the night?"

"Not till . . ."

"Yes, Miss Stayer?"

"Not till the morning."

"Who came then?"

"I don't remember."

"Who usually came?"

"Well, no one. I was nearly always the first up. I would get Aunt Lillianne's breakfast."

"But that morning someone did come to your room?"

"Yes. It was Babs. I remember now."

"Was Mrs Bomberger the only member of the household who took sleeping-pills?"

"Well, proper sleeping-pills, yes."

Carolus smiled.

"What are 'proper sleeping-pills'?" he asked.

"I mean, Aunt Lillianne had them prescribed by Dr Flitcher. They were terribly expensive. He prescribed some others for us called Komatoza. For Babs and me, that was."

"Were they effective?"

"Well, to tell you the truth, Mr Deene, we sometimes believed they were just as good as Aunt Lillianne's, though they cost a tenth of the price. They looked just the same, anyway."

"Oh. Did Miss Pink take any?"

"Well, yes. You know life with Aunt Lillianne was rather a strain, and I think we all felt we needed a little help to sleep at night. She took something quite different called Bromaloid, which was in liquid form."

"I see. So only you and your sister took Komatoza?"

"That's right."

"How many did you take?"

"The chemist said it didn't matter up to six or so. But we never took more than two each."

"You bought them from the chemist who made up your aunt's?"

"Cupperly's. Yes. Where I bought the weed-killer. You still haven't told me what to do about that."

"I have, Miss Stayer. I have told you to be frank."

"Yes. But why do they keep on now? Why, Mr Deene? They know Aunt Lillianne was not poisoned by weed-killer. Why do they keep asking me questions?"

"I can't tell you that. But you say you have nothing to conceal, so I should not worry any more. Tell me, Miss Stayer, have any of you ever been down to the beach at night?"

The last of Gracie's self-control broke at his question. Through angry tears she almost shouted, "No! no! Why do you ask such questions? We never went out at night. Scarcely into the garden, even. Aunt Lillianne did *once* want to be wheeled into the garden by moonlight, but never more than once. And never farther than the garden. Why do you ask? What *right* have you to ask?"

"No right at all. I only wanted to know whether the beach in Trumbles Bay was customarily quite deserted at night."

"Oh, quite. I should think, that is. I've never been down there."

"So that if Mrs Bomberger walked down herself to the beach that night, or if she was decoyed there, or wheeled there in her chair, or died first and was taken there—however she got there, in fact, no one need have seen it? No one, unless someone took her?"

"I suppose . . . oh, it's dreadful! There was no one about. There can have been no one about. We should have heard. It would have come out at the inquest. However she got there, there was no one to see, I'm sure."

"How do you think she got there, Miss Stayer?"

"I'm beginning to think she must have walked there. To meet someone, perhaps. There was that phone call."

"But that can't have been so very unusual. Mrs Bomberger must have had calls from people whose names you don't know?"

"Yes. Sometimes. But it was so extraordinary coming on the very night."

"You think she went down to the beach to meet this man who called himself Green and that he murdered her?"

"I know it sounds extraordinary."

"She is supposed to have died of an overdose of sleeping-pills."

"I don't see how they can tell. She had been in the water for hours. Suppose he made her unconscious in some way, then buried her up to the neck and let the tide drown her?"

"It's not a nice thought."

"It's horrible. But then the whole thing is horrible. And my aunt, let's face it, was a very horrible woman."

Carolus felt that Gracie at last was 'being herself'.

"You've no idea who 'Green' might be?"

"We've thought about that. There was a Mr Green with her publishers at one time, but we can't think it was him. Very quiet man who worked in the production department and had to see Aunt Lillianne about a dust-jacket she didn't like. But he left and went to some other publishers. I'm sure it wasn't him."

"In fact, Miss Stayer, you have nothing else to tell me?"

"Well, Mr Stump came up to the house that evening. Just before the phone call, I think. Or was it just after?"

"Did he see Mrs Bomberger?"

"Not that we know of. There had been a terrible quarrel between them and my aunt had given orders that Mr Stump was not to be admitted. Miss Pink opened the door and refused to let him in."

"I see. Anything else?"

"Not that I can think of. Unless you would like to see Aunt Lillianne's room or anything? It's all been cleaned up now."

"No. I won't trouble you to show me that. I should like to come out again tomorrow if I may?"

"Yes, yes. Do. Mr Deene . . ."

Carolus looked at the unhappy young woman quite steadily.

"Mr Deene, I feel I can trust you. Even if you did find out something I . . . we . . . if . . ."

"Miss Stayer, I shall sound very priggish and pompous, but with all my heart I recommend you not to hold back information in this matter. Whoever and whatever it may involve. I will see you tomorrow."

Carolus escaped with Fay without having to see Babs and Alice Pink again.

"What do you think of them?" said Fay as he drove back to Blessington.

"Fools. Worse. Oh, Fay, why do people, people of the kind we know and understand, commit murder? Anything rather than that. Surely. Starvation, misery, even death better than the curse of Cain. Sorry, my dear. I'm being portentous. Come and see whether Mrs Stick has managed to turn round sufficiently to give us dinner."

Priggley awaited them in a 'front room' from which

sufficient furniture had been cleared to admit the three of them.

"You didn't tell me you were going out to Bomberger's," he complained. "However, I've improved the shining hour."

"One of the forward and dizzy young women you call pieces of homework, I suppose?"

"That's a corny term, anyway. No, I was interested in Beddoes Farm. I decided to have a look round on my own. I left the bike a mile away and actually walked to the place. *Walked*, on my two feet. Is that devotion to duty?"

"You had no business to go out there again."

"I found chummy just finishing his job of changing the hand-brake cable."

"He saw you?"

"Certainly not. If he had I was going to ask for work on the farm during my summer holidays. There *are* unbelievable drears from squalid schools calling themselves the Public Schools Farmers' Aid, or some such thing. They actually plough and whatnot, I believe. So mine would have been quite plausible. But he didn't see me. On the contrary, I saw him. He picked up the old cable from where he'd chucked it and with it in his hand started off on foot from the shed. It was getting slightly duskish, but not nearly dark enough. I had to stay where I was and watch him across country. He made for a group of trees. I'm sorry if this all sounds nauseatingly R. L. Stevenson or John Buchan or something. I assure you, I don't want to be a Mountie. Too ludicrous. But I did go across to that group of trees afterwards. And what do you think I found? said little Red Riding Hood. A pond, Carolus. That character with the worn cable had felt strongly enough about it to walk across two fields and chuck it in a pond. Now, congratulations to me, and for God's sake let's have a drink."

7

Mrs Stick had indeed managed to 'turn round', for at that moment she came in to ask how many there would be for dinner.

"Can we manage three, Mrs Stick? Or am I asking too much on the day of your arrival?"

"If it's for Miss Fay and this young gentleman we can do it, sir. I'm not saying there would be enough for anyone . . ."

"Quite. Yes, it's for the three of us here. By what euphemism you speak of a 'young gentleman' I cannot think."

There was some discussion among the three of them after Mrs Stick had left the room as to whether that desiccated pucker round her mouth had been a smile. If so, it was unprecedented.

"Oh, by the way, sir, the creature with the bangles wants to speak to you. 'Please tell Mr Deene Ey shall be on duty tonate and have something to tell him.' "

Carolus sighed.

"Couldn't you get it out of her?"

"I tried, but no. 'Ey'm sorry et's a confeydential metter.' "

"That's the hell of this sort of job. One just can't afford to risk it. It's probably that her young man wants to be a detective, but it might be something. I'll walk back to the hotel with you later."

Mrs Stick gave them grilled lamb chops and a cheese *soufflé*. They spoke no more of the case while they were eating this, but afterwards Fay returned to the subject of Gracie.

"She's frightened," said Carolus. "A very frightened young woman."

"I know. I should think most people would be when they're interrogated so much. I rather like Gracie. I'm very, very sorry for her."

"Sure you're not confusing the two?"

"I suppose you will tackle Babs tomorrow?"

"I suppose so. Though I don't expect a lot from her. Or Alice Pink."

Under a brilliant August moon Carolus and Priggley walked round to the Royal Hydro, passing along the promenade among the holiday-makers.

'The creature with the bangles' smiled from behind her desk when she saw Carolus approach alone.

"Ey'm sorry you hevvn't stayed with us, Mr Deene. Ey feel there mate have been so many little theengs for you to observe here."

"You wanted to see me?"

"Yase, Mr Deene. A metter Ey feel Ey should tell you about. An individual keem here this morning and meed enquiries about you."

"Can you describe him?"

"Ey theenk so. He was a very shifty-looking individual. He hed a pronounced squeent."

"What? Oh yes, I understand. Gold teeth, had he?"

"How deed you know that? Ey suppose thet's being a detective. Yase. Several noticeable gold teeth. A tall individual. Most disagreeable. In fect, Mr Deene, hed it not been a metter which Ey thought mate interest you Ey should not have conversed with heem."

"What did he want to know?"

"He appeared to have gethered thet you were in some way interested in the kees. He weeshed to know who you were and what mate your connection be. Ey expleened to him thet you were a very feemous invest-igator."

"What did he say to that?"

"He smeeled and said, "Oh is thet all?' Ey said no more."

"Thenk . . . thank you for letting me know."

"Oh, nut et all. Ey'm most enterested. Ey faind et fescinating."

Next day Carolus rose to face what he knew would be a tough day's work. He had to go out to Trumbles as though it were his place of business. The interrogations with which he started his cases were often the most vital part of them and revealed the facts on which he based his later theory. 'Where were you at the time of the murder?' was something more than a cliché in these interrogations, it was a cogent and vital question and the answer to it might be the means of hanging a man. But all this meant hard work, and as he looked at his list of those he must interview at Trumbles he wondered whether after all detection for its own sake was worth while. Babs Stayer, Alice Pink, Graveston, Mrs Plum and Primmley the gardener. Then later George Stump, Dr Flitcher, Mr Cupperly, Harry Green, old Uncle Tom Cobley and all. But he would finish with Trumbles first, for if the idea that was beginning to take the first wisp of shape in his mind had any truth in it, it was at Trumbles that he would learn everything.

He started with Babs Stayer. Of the three women she was, he quickly realized, the least broken by life with Lillianne Bomberger and the least frightened by all that had happened since Lillianne's death. She was a dumpy, downright girl who if she had been left in her natural surroundings would have been 'a good sport' and 'great fun', if not 'the life and soul of the party'. She was not handsome, but she had a round face and good complexion; again one guessed what she would have looked like in other circumstances, a jolly, carefree, rather brazenly pretty girl.

She lit a cigarette.

"Shoot," she invited.

"All right. Let's start with the immemorial one. Where were you at the time of the murder?"

"Do we know what that was? Do we even know there was a murder?"

"We know that Mrs Bomberger was dead before the tide reached her. We know therefore that she died between eleven and three. In fact we can be more accurate than that, but let's take those as limits. Where were you between those times?"

"I went up to bed about eleven because poor Pink was fussing about the lights. I was reading for a bit . . ."

"What?"

"*Not* one of Aunt Lillianne's books. It was something George Stump brought down in proof. You know my aunt insisted on seeing everything on the same publisher's list as her books, and Stump and Agincourt used to send them down as bound proofs. I did not want to take any sleeping-pills, so I had chosen this as a bromide. It was enormously successful as that. I was asleep in two pages."

"What was the title?"

"Something about a mortar-board by someone called Porringer."

"*The Wayward Mortar-board*, by Hugh Gorringer."

"Oh, you know the book?"

"No. The man. Please go on."

"As I say, it put me out like a light and I slept right through to the morning."

"Was that unusual?"

"Not if I'd taken Komatoza."

"Do you usually take that?"

"Most nights if I'd seen much of Lillianne during the day. It was the only way I knew to rest my nerves."

"So nothing disturbed you that night?"

"Not a thing."

"What woke you in the morning?"

"Nothing. I slept right on."

"But your sister says you called her."

"Does she? I expect she's right. It's not very important."

"I'm sorry to be so trite, but it's really quite important.

It's an inconsistency, in fact a contradiction, and they are nearly always important. You say you slept right on till . . . ?"

"It must have been nearly eleven. I should think."

"What woke you then?"

"Mrs Plum. Telling me that Lillianne had been found dead on the beach, and the police were here."

"So that you slept the clock round? From eleven to eleven?"

"Yes."

"And that is where the contradiction comes in, Miss Stayer. You must forgive me for being so interested in it. Your sister says you came into her room quite early that day and woke her, though usually it was she who woke you."

"Could be. I've got an appalling memory. I may have got up that morning and made a cup of tea and taken her one, then gone back to bed."

"But you can't remember doing it?"

"No. I'm afraid I can't."

"Wasn't it unusual for someone who frequently has to take sleeping-pills to sleep twelve hours like that?"

Babs shrugged.

"You should know," she said.

"There's another matter on which you may be able to give me some information. I understand that it was you who supplied Mrs Bomberger with her sleeping-pills?"

"That's right. So far as anyone was responsible for the pills she took, I was. I had the prescriptions made up for her. But she never discussed them with me. She seemed to have a thing about them—secretive, you know."

"You told her how many she should take?"

"That was easy. Dr Flitcher and the chemist both emphasized that she should never have more than one at a time. They had morphine in them."

"Did your sister and Miss Pink know she was taking them?"

64

"I think so, vaguely. But neither had anything to do with it."

"But did you give them to her at night?"

"No one gave her anything. She kept her pills in the cupboard in her room and took them as she needed them."

"Was it your habit to go into her room at night?"

"Yes. When she was in bed. She was usually the first to go up, and I'd pop in to see if she wanted anything. She nearly always did."

"But not her sleeping-pills?"

"Just lately she had been right off them. 'If I *can* snatch a few hours of dozing without narcotics it is so much better for me. But I don't expect you to be interested in that. You have your own absorbing affairs.' "

"And had you?"

"What?"

"Affairs?"

"Singular, please. Yes, I've been in love with someone for a year, but he doesn't come into this."

"You'd rather not say who it is?"

"Oh, I don't mind, now. His name is Mike Liggott and he's a black-and-white artist working for an advertising agency. I met him on the beach last year and scarcely saw him again till his holiday this year. A fortnight ago we became engaged."

"Your aunt did not know, of course?"

"Not? Don't be absurd. There was nothing Lillianne did not know about anyone round her."

"But how?"

"Pink, I suppose. I don't altogether blame the wretched woman. She was terrified of Lillianne."

"How did your aunt take it?"

"How do you think? Behaved as though I was a school-girl caught writing rude things on the lavatory wall. Talked about 'vulgar intrigue' and 'servant-girl romance'. Forbade me to see Mike."

"But you continued to do so?"

"Secretly, yes."

"You intended to marry him in spite of your aunt."

Babs paused then said "Ye . . . es," rather dubiously.

"Surely there was no doubt about it?"

"You did not know my aunt," said Babs sulkily.

"But she couldn't prevent your marriage?"

"I would not put it past her."

"How?"

Babs was silent.

"Please, Miss Stayer, explain this to me."

"I'm over twenty-one, and she was not my guardian, anyway. But you just did not know that woman. If her own comfort was threatened, and her own domination of those about her, she would find a way."

"I can see that she would try. But I cannot see any way. Unless there was anything she could have said to your fiancé . . ."

"She would have found a way. But that is only one of the reasons I can't feel sorry—I know I ought to—I *cannot* feel sorry about her death."

"There are just one or two odds and ends of questions I want to ask you," said Carolus. He looked at a piece of paper, then, watching Babs carefully, asked, "Do you happen to remember what shoes your sister was wearing on the night of your aunt's death?"

Babs was unnaturally cool, and Carolus gathered that, as he had anticipated, the answer was prepared.

"Yes. But I bet she can't. She never remembers what she puts on. She was wearing a dreadful old pair of black velvet shoes. Really, a disgrace."

"She said they were nearly new."

Babs laughed.

"She wouldn't have the remotest idea. My sister and her clothes are a family joke."

Carolus found the idea of a joke in this family almost incredible.

"I told her a few days ago that she really must get rid

of the things. She wanted to give them to Mrs Plum, but I told her she'd be offended. 'Chuck them in the dust-bin,' I said, 'and if Plum wants them she can take them.' That's what she did, but I don't suppose she remembers even that."

"What shoes were you wearing?"

"What is all this about shoes? I mean, I'm quite willing to answer your questions if it will help you find out whether anyone actually killed Lillianne or not, and if so, who it was. But I can't for the life of me see what my shoes and Gracie's have to do with it."

"They have, you know."

"Oh, all right. I was wearing some rather pretty green leather shoes that evening. Want to see them?"

"No, thanks. Just one other thing. How many Komatoza tablets were you in the habit of taking?"

"Why?"

"It's a small point. Don't answer if you don't wish to."

"I'll answer. But this is really the oddest cross-examination. You haven't asked me a thing about Lillianne. I sometimes took several. Three or four."

"No more?"

"I might once or twice have taken a second lot in the night."

"Thank you."

"Now suppose you answer me a few questions," said Babs Stayer. "Was Lillianne murdered?"

"I don't know yet."

"Why was she half buried on the beach?"

"I'm not being evasive, but I don't know that, either. It's the key to the whole thing. I hope to be able to tell you in time. I'm really only getting my bearings."

"Do you want to see anyone else here?"

"Yes. Miss Pink. But I should like to come out this afternoon and see her. I have to go into Blessington now."

"Right. I'll tell her."

"Thank you."

"It seems to me, Mr Deene, that you're missing a couple

67

of important points. Two things happened that evening which were most unusual. George Stump called and was not admitted. And there was a phone call from someone who called himself Green."

"I've got details about both of those."

"You don't think they had anything to do with my aunt's death?"

"I haven't an opinion to express," said Carolus.

"Cagey, eh? Have a drink before you go?"

"No, thanks. I must run."

He said he knew his way to the car and took his leave. As he went round to the side of the house where the car was he had to pass a small open window. When he was near it he heard someone making a hissing noise like an infuriated snake.

"Psst! Here, I've got something to tell you."

Carolus didn't turn his head, but pretended to be viewing the garden. The hoarse, conspiratorial woman's voice continued:

"That's right. Don't turn round. I don't want them to know I'm speaking to you, only when you hear what I've got to say it'll stand your hair on end. I've seen things in this house to make your flesh creep. Things that would keep you awake at night. When I tell you everything you won't know whether you're coming or going. Only I can't stop now because one of them'll be out in a minute."

Carolus did not answer or turn, but nodded his head.

"I oblige here," the voice croaked on. "Mrs Plum. Haven't I seen your car in Sandringham Terrace? I thought it was the same one. It's almost next door to where I live. I know where you are. I don't know her to speak to, but I've seen her about for years. Well, I live at number thirty-seven. If you like to pop in there this evening when I get back from work I'll tell you something that will give you a nasty turn. If you was to know all I do you'd never feel the same again. Ssss. One of them's coming. See you this evening."

Carolus walked on. Before returning to Wee Hoosie, however, he sent a telegram to a man in London who had several times obtained for him supplementary information about persons in his cases. *Please obtain fullest details parentage record background of Cribb family of whom Lillianne Bomberger was daughter. Believe some still living Forest Hill.*

Then, exhausted and hungry, he went to see what Mrs Stick would give him for lunch.

8

CAROLUS decided to postpone his interview with Alice
Pink until after he had seen the secretive Mrs Plum and felt
some of the remarkable physical effects which she had
promised him. He had often wanted to know what creeping
flesh was and how his hair could be made to stand on end
except by a crew cut.

So after lunch he telephoned a postponement of his visit
to Miss Pink and went for a swim with Fay and Priggley.

"You're slacking, sir," said Priggley. "You can't let up
in the middle of a case like this. In fact I think your whole
handling of the thing is a bit corny."

"You do?"

"Certainly. After all, the old kind of detection's on its
way out. We've gone forward from Baker Street. I don't
see how you expect to get away with a mysterious murder,
examination of suspects, digging up the clues, keeping
everyone in the dark, then Bang, the big revelation. It was
all right for the first fifty years or so, but it's completely
outmoded now."

"Really? And how do you think I should deal with my
cases?"

"Far more suspense. Personal danger the whole time.
The American school. You start with being shot at as you're
walking home, long before you're investigating anything.
Then a touch of the macabre—a brace of human skeletons
in your bed at night. Rumours of great and gruesome
organizations working. Odd little things like a woman at a
bar suddenly screaming with terror. Pile it on. You might
get filmed or anyway televised. As it is you're dated, sir,
honestly."

"Thank you, Priggley."

"I'm not denying that you have a certain flair. You do seem to stumble on the truth at the end. But I find it all too staid and sticky. Look at you now, lying out here sunbathing. You ought to be up and being shot at somewhere."

"Carolus," said Fay. "There's that character."

"Allowing for your vagueness, Fay . . ."

"No. Really. You know the one. When we were driving up to the house. They swore they'd never heard of him. Gold teeth. Squint. You remember?"

"Oh yes. Walking along the lower promenade behind us?"

"Yes, just level with us now. He's not looking for anyone, I think. Just strolling."

"There you are, Priggley. Instead of talking so much, tail that oaf. Let me know where he stays."

There was no sign of the blasé young man in Priggley as he dashed off.

"Watch him till I'm dressed," he told Fay.

He was back in a moment and presently, when the man moved on, he followed.

Carolus lit a cigarette, and when the sun began to drop he and Fay left the beach.

At five o'clock he knocked at 37 Sandringham Terrace, envying Mrs Plum her simple digits. When she came to the door he saw her for the first time, a scrawny little woman with hispid upper lip and chin and an expression which suggested that her life was passed among the darkest mysteries and her nights were full of horror.

"Come in," she whispered, keeping herself half concealed behind her door. "No one's seen you, have they?"

"I think the woman who lives next door to me happened to be looking out as I passed."

"Oh, she was, was she?" hissed Mrs Plum. "From behind the blinds, you mean? She doesn't miss much. Mrs James, her name is, and she's very thick with the one where you are. Oh, very thick they are."

"I haven't seen my landlady," admitted Carolus.

"No. You wouldn't," said Mrs Plum. "She keeps herself to herself."

"Is she Scottish?"

"Not that I know of. What makes you ask?"

"The name of the house."

"That was there before her time. It's number thirty-one, if the truth were told. Now you want to know about Trumbles. Only I'm not supposed to Speak. They said there would be a bit of extra if I managed to keep my mouth shut, which I did with the nosy coppers. But when I heard a gentleman as was a gentleman had come to ask questions, and not them lousy narks, I thought I better say what I know, though it chokes me. You won't believe the half of it. It isn't as though I haven't got nothing to tell, either, because when you hear some of the things, I know you'll go white as a sheet. You'll shake in your shoes. You'll be struck all of a heap. I know you will. Only them having said it would mean a little extra *not* to talk I thought, well, there you are."

And there was Carolus handing over a pound note with great scepticism.

They were in a little room which corresponded to the 'front' one in Carolus's house, but here there were bamboo tables and large, dusty ferns. Carolus sat in one straight chair and Mrs Plum in another.

"I've read about such goings-on in the papers, but I never thought it would be where I was working. Some of the things will make your blood run cold. When you're working in a house like that with people you can't help hearing and seeing, and I tell you it will chill your spine. When I first come to realize what was going on I trembled all over like a haspin leaf . . ."

"Yes, yes. What did you notice?"

"I'll tell you one thing. They *hated* that Mrs Bomberger. Hated her so that they didn't hardly know what to do. Real hate it was."

"I know."

"Ah, but you don't know. Not like I do. If you could have seen their eyes sometimes. Like coals of fire, they was. And she just went on being sarcastic with them as though she didn't care how much it made them feel small. I tell you it gave me the creeps. It was as much as I could do to get through my work."

"Did you see any particular act which made you feel this?"

"Hundreds. What would you call it when Babs picked up the carving-knife and told me to take it with me and have it sharpened because it was blunt?"

"Was it?"

"I'm not saying it was like a razor, but when she said that to me it took my breath away. I began to be afraid of my own shadow. Then that Alice Pink putting things in Mrs Bomberger's coffee before she took it up in the morning."

"What sort of things?"

"Saccharine, she said it was, but when I saw her it turned me over inside. I thought I should go out of my wits. But what really gave me the horrors was that Graveston."

"I haven't seen him yet. He was the odd man, wasn't he?"

"You may well say it. He was the oddest man I've ever seen, and I've known a few. He used to push her up to the top of the cliff in her bath-chair, and every time they went I never thought to see her back again. I could hear my teeth chattering at the thought of it. I couldn't sleep at night for seeing her go over the edge, bath-chair and all, and being dashed to pieces on the rocks three hundred feet below."

"But I understand that it was Mrs Bomberger who chose that way."

"Ah, but that was just his artfulness. He made her think he didn't like pushing her up there so that she should want it. There's no denying she was very contrary. Oh, very contrary, she was."

"Yes, but Graveston certainly didn't push her over the edge of the cliff."

"Not yet he hadn't done, but you never knew when he wouldn't, did you? Then I haven't told you about those Cribbs. If ever anyone had murder in his heart he had. Well, I wouldn't put it past both of them. I'll never forget one afternoon when I happened to be passing the door where they was and I heard him. 'It *can't* go on,' he said, just like that. 'It *can't* go on.' I thought to myself, no it can't, else you'll do some wicked evil thing and there'll you'll be. Mind you, I'm not saying she wasn't a difficult woman herself, Mrs Bomberger, though she never tried anything with me. I did my work and that was it. But being difficult's one thing and being murdered's another."

"Undoubtedly," said Carolus. "Now, Mrs Plum, I want you to try to remember the Thursday morning when you went up to the house and the police came to report that they had found Mrs Bomberger's body."

"Remember it? As if I should ever forget it to my dying day! It isn't as though I'd been used to anything like that, because I've never been one to have anything to do with policemen, and as for murder, well! I never thought I'd get over it. I was in such a state . . ."

"Yes, but tell me about it as it happened. What time did you reach the house?"

"I caught the eight o'clock bus as usual which passes the end of the lane. I got up there at half-past eight, and as soon as ever I opened the back door . . ."

"You had your own key?"

"Yes. As soon as ever I opened the back door I knew there was something wrong."

"What made you think that?"

"I just felt it."

"Nothing was unusual? Out of place?"

"Not at first, there wasn't. But when I went into the big sitting-room where they always sat at night, I thought, This is funny."

74

"What?"

"Well, there was usually some cups and glasses lying about. Used ash-trays and that. That morning it was just as though they'd never been in there. Or if they had, some-one had done the room before I arrived."

"Had you ever known that before?"

"Not in the three years I've worked there. And when I went out to the kitchen there was nothing in the sink. They always washed up the supper-things—I think she made them do that—but there was nothing brought out from the big room. So I thought, I'll just have a look at the cupboard where she keeps the drink, what there is, and bless me if the key wasn't in it. Now that *was* unusual, because no one could ever get hold of that key but Mrs Bomberger herself, and she kept it with her. I can't say what had gone from the bottles because I never got a sight of them, but I saw the whisky bottle on the shelf was empty."

"Please go on."

"By this time I was in a nice state, knowing what I did, and began to notice other things. Her bath-chair, for instance."

"Yes?"

"Well, Graveston used to keep it in a sort of extra scullery we've got, and there it was. But I'd seen it when he put it away the night before, and now it was different. Clean as a new pin. What do you think of that?"

"I think it's very interesting. What else?"

"Everyone seemed to be asleep. That wasn't unusual for Mrs Bomberger, because sometimes she lay in all day, and woe betide anyone who disturbed her before she rung her bell. But when I listened at the foot of the back stairs I could hear Graveston snoring and there wasn't a sound from the rest of the house. Still, I thought, it's no business of mine, and I started on my work as though nothing had happened.

"Graveston was the first to come down. Him and me never have a lot to say to one another, and that morning I

75

didn't think it my place to ask any questions. I was just wondering whether I should go up and call Miss Gracie when there was a rat-tat on the front door to wake the dead and I felt my heart jump into my mouth. No sooner had I gone out than there were the police, two of them in plain clothes. Talk about a shock! I thought I should have the convulsions."

"You let them in?"

"I was too upset to do anything else. 'You work here?' said one of them. I don't know what else he could have thought when there was me with the duster in my hand. Then he gave me the news about Mrs Bomberger and told me to go and call the household and bring them down. Shall I ever forget it? It was on the tip of my tongue to say I could have told them as much with what I'd seen in the house already, but I managed to hold myself in and went off to call them.

"Miss Gracie was crying and Babs as pale as a ghost; and those Cribbs! Well, they had call to be upset of course with them thinking their Auntie was safe asleep in her bed and all the time she was buried in the sand with only her head sticking out. The police said it would be enough if Mr Cribb was to go down and identify her, and it didn't seem ten minutes before they was back and starting their questions. On they went all that day, and I was wondering when my turn would come. I couldn't take a bite to eat, though I did make a cup of tea for them and took it up to find these policemen sitting there.

"They started on me that very day. How long had I worked there and what had I noticed, but I knew how to answer them. Upset I might be, but I wouldn't have coppers asking me this that and the other and I was very short with them. Oh, very short I was. 'I do my work', I said, 'and ask no questions, so there you are.' No, I'd never noticed anything. By the time I'd done with them you'd have thought it was the nicest household you could find."

"I think you should have told them what you told me."

"Not likely. Not to coppers, I wouldn't. Let them find out for themselves."

"Did you do Mrs Bomberger's room that day?"

"No. The next day. The police were in it all that day taking photographs and fingerprints and that."

"But on the following day they let you clean it?"

"Yes. I did. Well, no one else wouldn't have fancied doing it, would they?"

"The bed had been slept in?"

"Well, it looked like it. That's all I can say. She wore nice silk pyjamas and they was in a heap on a chair as though she'd got dressed in a hurry. I didn't look to see what clothes were missing, because I wouldn't have known, Miss Pink looking after all that."

"So that's really all you have to tell me, Mrs Plum?"

"All? Well, isn't it enough? I should have thought I'd told you enough to give you the willies for the rest of your life."

Carolus stood up.

"Perhaps I don't want them," he said. "You've certainly given me some valuable information. Have there been any unusual callers since then?"

"I don't know what you call unusual, but they've been coming, morning, noon and night ever since. Policemen, pressmen, I don't know what. There was one wanted to take my photograph, but I wouldn't have that. . . ."

"You didn't notice a man with a squint?"

Mrs Plum looked up.

"No. That I didn't. And I would have because my husband had a squint and I always say it's lucky. No, I can't say anyone with a squint has been up there."

"Rather noticeable gold teeth?"

"No. Not that either. Why, is he the murderer?"

"We don't know yet that there was a murderer."

"If there wasn't I'd like to know what she was doing out there buried up to the neck in sand."

"Thank you very much, Mrs Plum."

"If there's anything else, I'll tell you. I know where you are. She's lucky to have let that house, that's what I say. I can't think who else would have taken it with all that furniture. It looked to me like an auction sale whenever I passed the window. Still, she's a very respectable person, I will say that."

"Good night, Mrs Plum."

"Wait a minute. I'll come and see you out. I don't want half the street knowing you've been here."

Mrs Plum cautiously opened the front door and peered out.

"It's all right," she whispered; "only go the other way first and walk back in a few minutes as though you'd never been here. Her friend'll be watching, you may be sure of that, and it doesn't do to have talk. Good night."

Carolus did as he was told, and in a few minutes was back at Wee Hoosie, where Mrs Stick was waiting for him with her severest expression.

"There's been someone hanging round," she said. "I was afraid this would start, sir."

"What kind of person?"

"Not at all the sort of person Stick and me would expect to see where we work, sir. A nasty, trampy-looking man with a squint."

"Oh, that one," said Carolus. "Did he come to the door?"

"I should think not," said Mrs Stick. "Your dinner will be ready in twenty minutes."

9

"Miss Pink," said Carolus firmly when he faced the Secretary next day, "if you are going to tell me that you went up to bed at eleven on the night of Mrs Bomberger's death, and slept until eleven the next morning without hearing anything in the night, don't let us waste our time talking. I know it's not true, and I'm tired of being told lies by people I'm supposed to help."

"I . . . really . . . I don't think you should speak to me like that. I haven't told you any lie."

"Yet," said Carolus. "But you were going to tell me the one I've just described."

"I scarcely know. . . . Perhaps it *would* be as well if you did not question me if it is going to be in this very hectoring manner."

"I'm sorry if I was rude," said Carolus. "But really it is rather exasperating to hear what one knows isn't true."

"I'm not the one. . . . Surely you should put your questions to Mrs Bomberger's nieces. Or to Mr Cribb."

Miss Pink writhed. One might almost use the dangerous adverb and say she 'literally' writhed. She twisted her thin body about on the settee in alarming nervousness.

"What time did you go to bed?"

"It must have been quite midnight. I had many little things to do before retiring. I like to tidy up."

"What was there to tidy up that evening? In the sitting-room where you had all been, I mean?"

"Oh, just glasses. A cup and saucer. Ash-trays. But I usually leave those on a tray for Mrs Plum in the morning. It is more the books and newspapers which I looked after. Mrs Bomberger was very particular about those."

79

"Were there glasses, cups and ash-trays in the big sitting-room that night?"

"Yes. *No!* No. None at all."

Carolus sighed.

"You see what I mean? You're determined not to tell me the truth. 'Yes', you said quite normally and of course truthfully. Six people had not spent three hours of an evening in a room without leaving them. 'Yes' was the truth. Then suddenly you remember something you have prepared yourself to say. Or been told to say. You shout 'No!' and now you're going to stick to it."

Miss Pink twirled and knotted herself desperately.

"There weren't any glasses. Not one. Nor ash-trays. I don't know why. Perhaps no one had smoked or had a drink or coffee. Perhaps they cleared up before they went to bed. There wasn't one!"

"Let's leave that. At last, at about midnight, having finished downstairs, you went up to your room?"

"Yes. It must have been."

"And then?"

"I retired," said Miss Pink bashfully.

"You didn't go first to Mrs Bomberger's room?"

"Just to the door. I heard her sleeping."

"You mean she snored?"

"Frequently, yes. That night it was just a light stertoration."

"So you didn't go in?"

"No."

"What next?"

"Well, nothing really. Sleep," said Miss Pink, adding in a dubious melancholy voice, "the cool kindliness of sheets that soon smooths away trouble."

"Bomberger?"

"No. Rupert Brooke."

"What awoke you?"

"Me? When? Oh, it's hard to say. I . . ."

"Come, Miss Pink. I've told you I won't listen to a

fairy tale about a beautiful night's sleep ending at eleven next morning."

"It was . . . I don't know the time . . . I had taken a drop of my Bromaloid, of course. I can't think . . ."

"Yes, you can. You're thinking now of what answer you should give. What happened during the night?"

"During the night?"

"You needn't sound as though the question was such an extraordinary one. After all, at some time during the night Mrs Bomberger, alive or dead, went or was taken from her bedroom to the beach. It isn't very surprising that I should ask you, who slept in the next room, what you heard of it."

"Oh that. Nothing, really. Mrs Bomberger could move very softly when she wished. I've *always* thought she left the house that night of her own volition."

"You're going to tell me you heard *nothing*?" asked Carolus savagely.

Miss Pink wilted, performed a couple of convolutions which a professional contortionist would have envied and seemed to think very hard.

"There was my dream, of course."

"I do not want to hear dreams. There is nothing in the whole world so boring as an account of someone's dream unless it's a story of the intelligence of his dog. I want to know what you heard or saw."

"It may not have been *quite* a dream," said Miss Pink coyly.

"You mean, it happened?"

"You shall hear for yourself. I am not really altogether certain. I went to sleep for a while and then—I scarcely know if I was awake or asleep—then I seemed to hear a voice."

"Whose?"

"Mrs Bomberger's."

"That must have been nice for you."

"On the contrary. I had had the experience before. She was a very domineering person, as no doubt you have

81

realized. More than once I had suffered from nightmares in which she was calling me insistently. On one or two occasions I went hastily to her room to see what she wanted. That made her most annoyed, because it was only my imagination and she wasn't calling me at all. This time it was different."

"In what way?"

"The call did not seem to come from her room."

"Where did it come from?"

"It seemed to be on the wind. 'A voice on the wind at even.'"

"Brooke?" said Carolus.

"No. Bomberger," admitted Miss Pink.

"How do you mean, 'on the wind'?"

"Out of the night, Mr Deene. 'A voice whose sound was like the sea.' That's Wordsworth."

"Was it like the sea?"

"It seemed to come from the sea. Or from near the sea. My window faced that way. It was a breezy night with no moonlight much. My window was open. 'Alice!' I seemed to hear. 'Alice!'"

"Seemed to hear or heard?"

"I can't quite draw the distinction. I am still not sure if I was asleep or awake. 'Alice!' it seemed to call in a sad, despairing way."

"So what did you do?"

"I was never quite awake, I think. The Bromaloid, you know. I must have dropped off properly."

"At what time did this happen? The voice, I mean?"

"Oh, I couldn't possibly say. I'm not even sure there was a voice."

"Then you slept till eleven and were woken by Mrs Plum saying the police were here? I've heard it all before."

"No. Not that," said Miss Pink confidentially. "As a matter of fact I did rather oversleep that morning. But I woke at ten. I looked at my watch and thought, I must get up quickly. Mrs Bomberger's bell might ring at any moment, and I had not sorted her post or prepared her breakfast or anything. I dressed as quickly as I could and was just going downstairs when Mrs Plum announced the police."

"It's a small variation," admitted Carolus.

"That's all I can remember of that night."

"What did you feel about Mrs Bomberger?"

"Feel about her? Oh. It's very hard to answer that. She was such a dominant personality. In a way I was most attached to her. I had been with her for ten years. But she was so overbearing. She had no respect for other people's feelings. She could treat one in the most humiliating way."

Carolus nodded slowly and said no more.

"It was you who answered the door to Mr Stump that evening?"

As though relieved at escaping from other topics, Miss Pink answered eagerly.

"Yes. And it was I who took that phone call from an unknown man."

Again Carolus was silent and again Miss Pink looked uncomfortable.

"Is that all you want to know?" she asked at last.

"No, Miss Pink, it is not. But it is all I have any intention of asking you. It is evidently not the slightest use expecting to hear the truth. 'All I want to know?' No. I want to know how Miss Stayer came to spoil a nearly new pair of black velvet shoes that night and why her sister lies about it. I want to know why the ash-trays and glasses were removed from the big sitting-room and cleaned at some time in the small hours. I want to know who took the key of the drinks cupboard from Mrs Bomberger's room and who drank the whisky."

Alice Pink gave a kind of convulsive jerk as each of Carolus's points went home. It was evident that she was near hysterics.

"I want to know who cleaned Mrs Bomberger's bath-chair and why? I want to know how Mrs Bomberger came to take that quantity of sleeping-pills and at what time she died. A great deal of this you could tell me, but you have decided not to. All right. I've warned all of you of the danger."

"Danger?"

"The danger of not speaking the truth when it's a matter of life and death. The danger of hoodwinking the police, who are the people responsible for your safety. The danger of concocting a wholly false and incomplete story and sticking to it through thick and thin. The danger of a conspiracy, Miss Pink. Of a conspiracy."

Miss Pink had twisted herself so violently during these last words that Carolus was becoming quite alarmed. However, she found a safety-valve by bursting into tears and dashing from the room.

Carolus remained alone for a time, smoking and thinking. From the window he saw Primmley the gardener at work and remembered that he had to interview him and Graveston. But he felt disinclined to ask more questions at present. He was, as he had rather brutally told Miss Pink, tired of hearing lies.

However, he was not given a respite, for there was a tap at the door, followed by the entrance of Graveston.

Mrs Plum had described him as the oddest man she had ever seen, and it may well have been no exaggeration. Tall and lugubrious, he was dressed in a dark suit and wore a starched collar and black tie. The top of his head was bald but, as though ironically, hair grew with uncontrolled luxuriance elsewhere about him, his eyebrows beetled, his ears were the pink environments of tangled brush, his nostrils bristled, the backs of his hands were dark with wiry growth. From the depths of his long throat came a cavernous voice.

"I understand you want to question me, sir. I'm not at liberty to tell you much."

"What on earth do you mean?"

"I have my duty. I know what is right and what is wrong."

"You're a lucky man."

"I was strictly brought up. My father used to say, 'Now you know the difference between Right and Wrong. Do Right.' "

"And did you?"

"I did, sir. I have no intention of doing other. That is why I say I am not at liberty to tell you everything you may wish to know."

"I see. I suppose we start with the old grind about you going to bed at eleven and sleeping until eleven o'clock next morning?"

"That would be inaccurate, sir. I should not wish to say anything like that. What I say will be right. I did not reach the house till nearly one o'clock in the morning."

Carolus sat up.

"Oh, you were *out* that evening?"

"I was, sir. It wouldn't be right for me to say anything else."

"May I ask where you were?"

"At a meeting of the Elders of the Mount Sion Revealed Persuasion and Band of Charity. We have our little meeting-place in Blessington. You may have noticed it? A red-brick building opposite the old fish market."

"That kept you late?"

"I knew that the last bus left at ten, but I felt it was only right to stay to the end of the meeting. So I walked home."

"Did you go straight to bed?"

"I felt I owed it to myself to make a cup of tea before doing so. I should not wish to deny that."

"So it must have been half-past one before you were finally between the sheets?"

"I should not for a moment claim such accuracy. I cannot be sure just what time I went to bed and would not pretend to. But if I may guess I should say it was about then, about one-thirty."

"Which way did you come home?"

Graveston appeared startled by the simple question.

"I hardly feel called upon . . ." he began.

But Carolus interrupted sharply.

"Nonsense. There are three ways you could have come from Blessington: along the sands, over the cliffs or inland by the road. Which did you take?"

Graveston did not move a muscle, yet Carolus felt that his inner writhings were no less than Miss Pink's outward ones had been.

"It's not for me . . ."

"Which one?"

"Along the sands. I wouldn't tell you anything else."

"You didn't want to tell me at all. Why not?"

"I want to do right. I . . ."

"Oh, very well. Did you meet anyone as you came that way?"

"Several persons. Two courting couples I remember distinctly because I couldn't approve of their attitudes."

"No one you knew?"

"No, sir."

"You're sure you came by the sands, Graveston?"

"I certainly should not say so if I wasn't. I should not feel it right to deceive you on any point, though there may be some questions I cannot answer."

"So your shoes must have been sandy when you came in?"

"I had been walking on dry sand above high-water mark. This would not cling to boots at all."

"No. That is what I was thinking. If any of your shoes were wet, salty or clogged with sand it must have been from another excursion that night?"

Graveston blinked, but remained silent.

"Did you go out again that night, Graveston?"

"I went to bed, sir. I can't pretend I didn't."

"But did you get up again?"

"To answer a call of Nature—yes, sir."

"You did not leave the house?"

"No."

"You do not know whether anyone else did?"

"On such matters I cannot speak, sir. It would not be right for me to do so."

"You sleep deeply?"

"No, sir. I cannot go so far as that. I slept fitfully."

"When did you clean Mrs Bomberger's bath-chair?"

"I am unable to say, sir. I cleaned it whenever it was necessary, that is all I can tell you."

"You had recently formed a habit of taking Mrs Bomberger to the top of the cliffs?"

"It was the lady's wish to go that way."

"Did you ever think how easy it would be for you to let the bath-chair run over?"

"Such thoughts would never enter my head. I should not think it right to contemplate a possibility like that."

"We can't always control our thoughts. But we can be honest with ourselves about them. All right, Graveston. You have resolved not to tell me the truth. I shan't ask you any more. But I warn you that if you have told the same lies to the police as you have to me you're in danger of immediate arrest on a charge of murder."

"Me, sir? That couldn't possibly be. I had nothing whatever to do with it."

"With what?" shouted Carolus.

"With the death of Mrs Bomberger. I understand the lady died from an over-dose of sleeping-pills."

"Why did you clean that bath-chair in the small hours of that morning?"

"I did no such thing. I can say no more."

Carolus sent him to ask Gracie and Babs Stayer and Miss Pink if they could see him and in a few moments the household was gathered. Carolus spoke very briefly.

"I have no more enquiries to make here," he said, "and

I am delighted that it is so. I do not know why you told my cousin you wanted me to investigate if you were not going to give me the facts. I feel it is only fair to warn you, and I hope you will pass the warning on to Mr and Mrs Cribb, that you all, and particularly one of you, that you *all* are in danger. Neither I nor the police can do anything for you while you persist in keeping us in the dark."

"Danger? Of what?" asked Gracie.

"Death," said Carolus and left them. He went quickly to his car and drove back to Blessington.

10

PRIGGLEY was waiting for him.

"I trust you'll never again expect me to do anything quite so banal as that," he said in a bored voice, apparently referring to the task given him yesterday. "Shadowing a man with a squint! Really, I might be Valentine Vox, or something. Won't you ever grow up, sir?"

"You thoroughly enjoyed it," said Carolus. "What's more, you've probably done it extremely well. Let's hear about it."

"Are you giving me lunch? I'm beginning to find that the *table d'hôte* in the Grand Restaurant Romano-Ritz at the Royal Hydro, to say the least of it, *palls*."

"You'd better ask Mrs Stick."

"Easy," said Rupert and went out to the kitchen. In a few moments he returned in triumph. "Though she says 'Mind you, if it had been one of them mixed up with this nasty business there wouldn't have been, and I don't mind if Mr Deene knows it.'"

Rupert poured out sherry for Carolus and himself, sniffing appreciatively over the glass before almost gargling with the wine as he swallowed, in the manner of a professional taster. It was clear that he believed he had a good story and did not intend to be hurried.

"That's a squalid character," he said at last. "Insults-to-women stuff. You know, walks along, sees a decent woman out shopping or what-have-you, and just says something nasty to her as he passes. Walking behind him made me quite ill. Each time he passed a woman alone I would see him stoop towards her and then watch her colour up and hurry on."

"It's quite common," said Carolus, "and very hard to deal with, because the women hate complaining, which entails repeating what the man has said. Very unpleasant. Go on."

"He led me all over the town on this, and I was just going to let him go to hell and tell you to find someone else for the job when he looked at his watch. I guessed he had made a decision to go home, and I was right. He disappeared into *Peep O'Day, Board Residence, Sorry We're Full, Write Next Year,* 16 Windsor Terrace. I went and had a cup of tea at the café on the corner, from which I could see the entrance of his place. I was sure he had not had enough amusement for the day and waited for him to come out. It took about an hour and I was getting pretty bored with a rather dreary blonde behind the counter of my café before I saw him slope into the evening air. I waited till he was well out of sight, then went over to Peep O'Day and asked for the proprietress.

" 'We're full up,' said a bright little woman with a grey fringe. 'I know. I'll write next year,' I told her. 'I wanted to see you about something else.' She seemed a bit doubtful, but eventually asked me into her kitchen. 'What is it?' she said; 'because I'm so busy I haven't time to turn round.' I didn't hedge. 'It's about that man who has just left,' I said, 'Squint. Gold teeth.' I could see at once that she had had her own doubts about our man. 'It's a bit difficult to explain, Mrs . . .' 'Salter,' she said. 'Mrs Salter. I'm afraid it may take a few minutes.' I'd got her curiosity thoroughly roused now. She wouldn't have let me out of that room for a fortune. 'Sit down,' she said.

"I gave her the works. Strictly true except that I invented a sister of mine who had been insulted. I intended to give the man a good hiding. 'Not in my house,' she stipulated, and I agreed. My sister would not let me go to the police, but I was thinking of other people's sisters, too, etcetera, etcetera. Mrs Salter came out with quite a lot. The man's name is Poxton and he has been here three weeks. He now owes one week's rent, but has promised the money tomorrow 'for certain, as he is receiving a large sum'. He doesn't come down to breakfast in the morning, though Mrs Salter doesn't 'do' breakfasts up in bedrooms. 'Well, I couldn't do it. Not when we're full up like this.' He 'lies in', as she says, until just on lunch-time, then goes round to the Feathers, and comes in late for lunch, which makes it so awkward for everybody. 'I've only got the one woman to help me and naturally we both want to get washed up.' In the afternoon he goes out as he did today.

"But it is his nocturnal movements which interest Mrs Salter. He's out, as she says, 'till all hours'. He has his key, as all the boarders at Peep O'Day have, and has come in as late as two o'clock in the morning. 'And after what you've told me,' said Mrs Salter, 'I don't dare to think what he may be up to.' I asked what time he usually goes out at night, and she says it is never before nine and usually between nine-thirty and ten. I thought of hanging about last night for him to emerge, but decided to wait till I had told you what I'd learnt."

"Good."

"I'll go tonight, shall I?"

"I shall go."

"But you'll let me come?"

"I'm afraid you would find it what you please to call corny, Priggley. Following a man by night."

"Of course it's corny. But corn can be fun. I'll call for you at eight forty-five."

"I don't think I'll take the responsibility."

"Oh, come off it, sir. It's not as though the man were a murder suspect."

"Why not?"

"He's just a repulsive cad who mumbles filth to women."

"That doesn't mean that he's not a suspect. Rather the contrary. You're far too apt to dismiss people from suspicion because there is this or that about them. A murder, this murder anyway . . ."

"If it *is* a murder . . ."

"If it is a murder, could be committed by almost anyone. Even by someone who appears merely funny like Mrs Plum, someone who seems the soul of ordinariness like Ron Cribb, someone frightened like Alice Pink, someone hysterical like Gracie Stayer, or someone downright like Babs Stayer. Besides more sinister characters like Graveston. It could be the work of an attractive woman like Gloria Cribb or a businessman like George Stump. It could certainly have been done by a nasty piece of work like this Poxton."

"I suppose so. Anyway, I'm coming. After all, we're in the holidays."

"Are you sure he didn't see you yesterday?"

"Certain. Part of his act was not to turn round when he had spoken to a woman. I kept well behind."

"That won't be so easy tonight."

"Why not? There's a full moon."

So at nine o'clock Carolus and Priggley had a coffee at the Kozee T Rooms on the corner of Windsor Terrace and Carolus had an opportunity of seeing the 'rather dreary blonde' described by Priggley. But that evening Priggley did not seem to find the lush young woman in the least dreary.

It was nearly ten o'clock before Poxton came out of Peep O'Day. Carolus saw now that he was a tall man, fairly heavily built. He wore a light raincoat and a colourless hat.

It soon became evident that he had some urgent objective. He showed no disposition to repeat his insulting behaviour of yesterday afternoon, but started to walk towards the sea without pausing anywhere.

It was, as Priggley had predicted, a night of good, strong moonlight, and the sea looked like the surface of the moon itself. The streets of the town were quite brightly lit, and while Poxton continued to walk along the promenade as he was doing it would be easy to keep him in sight from far enough away. When he left the range of the promenade lights there might be a problem.

The band was still playing in the pagoda-like bandstand, and although the evening was chilly the promenade was populous. 'Listening to the band' remained a beloved occupation in spite of all the counter attractions of the cinema, radio, television, not to mention public performances of music and drama. A great number of people spent a very happy hour or two shivering in uncomfortable and expensive deck-chairs while bandsmen in uniform beat out the traditional Selection from *Yeomen of the Guard* or something from *Peer Gynt*. Poxton led them right past the bandstand, and Carolus wondered if he could be aware that he was being followed and was trying to lose them. But no, he walked on steadily, heedless of the crowd as he was of the music. He was going northward.

When he came to the end of the promenade he did not hesitate a moment, but dropped to the sand below it. It now seemed certain that he was going to walk round the headland to Trumbles Bay.

"Pity we haven't got a football," said Carolus.

"I suppose you said what I thought I heard you say. Or am I going mad?" asked Priggley.

"I said a football. We could then have a jolly game dribbling and passing all round our man and he'd think nothing of it."

"Gosh, you're right. I'm relieved. For a moment I thought you were suffering from arrested development. Tell you what, we can fake up something to kick with litter rolled up. And heaven knows there's plenty of litter."

"You need some string."

"I've got some," said Priggley unexpectedly. "Don't you know it's one of the things every schoolboy carries in his pocket?"

In a few moments the ball was made. Carolus waited until Poxton would be well on his way round the headland, then, with a good deal of shouting and false merriment which Priggley particularly enjoyed, with cries of "Oh, good shot, sir!" "Rotten luck!" "Very hard lines!" and "Well played!" they passed Poxton. It was as well that they adopted these tactics, as Poxton, after leaving the promenade, gave frequent glances behind him to make sure he was not followed. Presently they reached the shadows of the rocks in Trumbles Bay. Here they took up their position and waited for their man to appear.

The whole bay was brightly lit by the moon except on the south side, which Carolus had chosen. Here were some tall stark rocks, and it was easy to remain invisible among them.

"But I think he'll go up to the house," said Carolus. "I suggest your getting there ahead of him. I'll wait here. See and hear all you can, but don't take risks. And don't leave the shadows on this side."

Priggley faded from sight within a few yards and Carolus cursed the inadvisability of lighting a cigarette. It was not many moments, however, before Poxton appeared and marched, as Carolus had anticipated, right across the middle of the bay towards the track which led up to Trumbles. When he too became invisible—at a much greater distance than Priggley, because he was in moon-light—Carolus could afford to enjoy his smoke.

It seemed to him, who was the least impatient of men, a very long time before anything happened. He consoled himself a little for the boredom of a long wait by thinking that if this went as he hoped it would bring him far nearer a solution than he had been at any time since the case began. With any luck he would at least know what had happened on this shore that night.

Priggley was suddenly beside him, a little out of breath.

"Pink the Secretary met him at the gate. They scarcely exchanged a word, but she handed him a packet. He'll be across in a minute."

"Right. Stay here. Understand?"

Priggley appeared to know when Carolus intended an order to be kept.

"Yes. I'll stay here till you shout for me."

Soon the tall figure was in sight, hurrying now.

Carolus walked out of the shadow.

"Poxton!" he said loudly.

Afterwards he decided that it was a ridiculous and exaggerated phrase, but at the time he thought Poxton stopped as though he had been shot.

"Who you talking to?"

"Blackmailing again?" said Carolus coldly.

"Who are you?"

"I'm not the Law, luckily for you. Hand over that packet."

"Who? . . . Oh, you're the amateur detective, are you? Hoping for a cut?"

"What an incredible fool you are, Poxton. Do you want to go inside again? Hand over that packet."

"What —— packet?"

"Must we go through all this? The packet that wretched woman's just given you."

"Not bloody likely!"

"You must know that I've got the number of every note in the lot and every one is marked. You wouldn't have spent six before you were picked up."

This seemed to impress Poxton.

"The lousy bitches," he said. "Is the Law in on this?"

"No. But they're going to be. Hand it over."

Carolus could not see the man's eyes, but he could almost hear his thoughts. Make a dash for it? Draw a chiv and silence Carolus for good? Brazen it out? Give in? It was probably the idea that the notes were useless which made him decide on the last.

He pulled a packet from his pocket and silently held it out.

"Now what had you got on them?"

"If I tell you that, will this go no farther?"

Carolus considered this. It was against his principles to let a blackmailer go free, but he badly wanted his information.

"What has happened tonight will go no farther," he said. "But I can't answer for the past. If you had any hand in the death of Mrs Bomberger or her burial here I'm not guaranteeing you any immunity. Nor will I try to cover you for not giving your information to the police. I will only give you my word that I will not expose you as a blackmailer on the strength of what you've done tonight."

"That'll do for me."

"What had you got on anyone, Poxton?"

"You want the truth?"

"Of course. Don't stall."

"All right. I'll tell you. Nothing. Sweet Fanny Adams."

"Nonsense. Even the Secretary wouldn't hand over money . . ."

"I'll tell you what I did. Read the case in the paper. Then used my loaf. Rang them up. Said I'd been having a walk along here that night and had seen everything. Everything, I said. Well, it stood to reason, didn't it? Someone must have brought her down here and buried her. I'd no idea who it was, but I guessed someone in that household had something to hide. It worked like a charm. I went up to see them one evening. They hadn't got any money there then, but they've managed to raise it. Five hundred nicker in one-pound notes."

With sick disappointment Carolus supposed that the man was telling the truth.

"You weren't even here that night?"

"I was in bed and asleep. I don't know from Adam who buried the woman or why. I know nothing about it."

Carolus looked at the man and felt a nausea and anger.

"Tell you what," Poxton said, "I've got to have a few quid to pay my digs. I promised it tomorrow."

"I'll ring up Mrs Salter in the morning and tell her that I'll be responsible for what you owe, but only if you're out of this town by eleven o'clock. If you're wanted for anything in connection with the case, the police can pick you up when they like."

96

He left Poxton and started to walk towards the rocks where Priggley was waiting. He turned to see Poxton hurrying on towards Blessington.

"All we know from that," he said disgustedly, "is what we knew already—that someone at Trumbles has a good deal to hide. I think I'm going to be sick."

"Poxton or disappointment?"

"Both."

"To think," said Priggley as they started for home—"to think that we've played beach football for nothing."

11

GEORGE STUMP, the famous and successful publisher, had not been given his nickname of 'Gobbler' Stump for nothing. He looked like a turkey-cock, with the same red face and floppy jowls, the same sharp nose and the same fixed rare-blinking stare of very round eyes. He was, moreover, a gobbler by nature. He gobbled up authors whom he thought worth while and gobbled the profits from their books; he gobbled up some excellent wines and gobbled down enormous lunches with his business associates. He had gobbled up Lillianne Bomberger when she was an unknown writer and found her the most indigestible though profitable thing he had ever gobbled in his life.

Carolus had left him to simmer uncomfortably at the Palatial Hotel, a rather dingy brick building near the station at which Lillianne had always booked him rooms when he was coming down. George Stump believed this to be a deliberate step to keep him in his place, the sort of thing Lillianne Bomberger was in the habit of doing. She did not pay his hotel bill, of course; the inference of her choice was that he would not wish and should not be able to afford the best.

Carolus had passed the Palatial several times, but had deliberately avoided an interview with the publisher. He felt that Stump would eventually volunteer information and then be more communicative than if Carolus went and pleaded for it.

On the day after his failure to learn anything worth while from Poxton Carolus received a short note.

Dear Deene,

    I believe you are a friend of my partner William Agincourt and that you are amusing yourself by investigating the death of Lillianne Bomberger. I don't know whether any information of mine can assist you but if you care to try, do come to dinner tonight at about eight and I will rake my memory.

Yours sincerely,
George Stump.

"Thank you for your kindness in offering me dinner and information," Carolus wrote back. "But I regret to say I'm already engaged this evening. Some other time, perhaps? I am sorry to have no telephone here."

This had the very effect he hoped. At four o'clock that afternoon Stump rang the bell at Wee Hoosie and was shown by an unsuspecting Mrs Stick into the crowded and stuffy front room.

"I was coming this way," said the publisher. "So I thought I'd look in and see when you're coming to dinner."

"Very kind of you," said Carolus.

"One day next week?"

"Delighted. Yes."

"Tuesday?"

"Thank you. Suits me splendidly."

Stump made no move from his chair.

"I understand you're going to have a book by my headmaster Hugh Gorringer on your Spring List." Carolus was being maddeningly irrelevant.

"Yes, yes. *The Wayward Mortar-board,*" said Stump hurriedly.

"Will you do well with it, do you think?"

"Quite safe, that sort of book. Couple of thousand copies. Old boys and that. Nothing like Bomberger."

"Nothing?"

"Sales, I meant. In dealings—well, now you suggest it, yes. There is a little something similar in the way they write . . . wrote to us. A little self-importance, perhaps."

Carolus smiled.

99

"Sad about Bomberger," said Stump, evidently determined not to let the name slip.

It was the first time Carolus had heard that adjective used about the novelist's death, and he felt it to be the merest hypocrisy.

"Very sad. You won't get rid of Gorringer so easily."

"*Get rid of?* What an unfortunate thing to say!"

"I meant that Gorringer will outlive us all. You'll find yourself publishing *Murmuring Labours*, a sequel to . . ."

"I hardly think so," Stump snapped. "Look here, Deene, are you going to find out the truth about this thing?"

"With luck, yes."

"I should like to be of any help I can."

"I don't know that there is much I need bother you with."

"I knew her very well."

"Oh yes?"

"Damn it, I ought to. She was with us for twenty-three years."

"I understand she was leaving you?"

"Who told you that? It's nonsense. She threatened to leave us every two months. This was a little more serious, but it would have come to no more than the other times."

"Tell me about it."

"It began nearly a year ago, when her last book came out, *Dying Violets*. We'd given it a very clever dust-jacket which was just what the trade wanted. Bit sensational, but a seller. Bomberger saw it and screamed. Literally, in my office. She wanted a design of actual dying violets, half-dead flowers. Can you imagine it? How would anyone buy a book with faded flowers all over it?"

"I should have thought that if they wanted a book with that title they wouldn't have minded the picture."

"But it's not titles that sell books, Mr Deene. No one remembers titles. Well, as I say, Bomberger wanted violets just as the book was going into print. I told her it was impossible. She said she'd take the book away from us. I said that was impossible, too, because she'd signed the contract. She swore she'd take her next novel to Peter Davies. I said she bloody well could. Let him have her, I said. I was sick of it. 'See if Peter Davies'll give you violets on your dust-jacket,' I said. Well, that's how it began. We'd had rows before, but they'd always been patched up. This time I sent her a big bunch of violets, but she sent them back."

"What happened about the dust-jacket?"

"I kept ours on."

"So she failed to get her own way. That was dangerous."

"Of course it was. We've had nothing but trouble since. She was a fiend about advertisements. She'd measure the type in which her name was printed and scream blue murder if she found Frances Parkinson Keyes or someone in larger letters. Bomberger was one of those authors whom you don't need to advertise. She sold herself. But we had to waste thousands on every book she did. Can you imagine advertising Bomberger in *The Times Literary Supplement*? That's what she wanted. But what could we do?"

"Get rid of her."

"That's what I decided to do, but Agincourt wouldn't have it. 'She's the goose that lays the golden eggs,'' he said. Let me tell you what happened. She sent us her next, *The Flower of Death*. She had to because we had an option. But I saw from the first that she was determined to make it impossible for us to publish it. She kept the proofs two months, then sent them back hacked to pieces. She turned down three jacket designs I sent her and demanded one by Augustus John or Francis Bacon. She disagreed with every publication date we proposed. Of course she had no legal right to do any of this, but we had always given her plenty of rope. Finally I decided to go ahead as we wanted and let her leave us. Peter Davies could have her for all I cared, though I'd never wish the Bomberger on anyone, even another publisher.

"When publication date approached she asked me to

come down to Blessington and talk things over. What else could I do?"

"You could have gone abroad."

"I honestly thought she wanted to make it up. And there's no doubt about it, she did sell. So I came down. I found not only that she hadn't relented, but that she was going to try to get her past books away from us, too. I didn't see how she could because I'd kept them all in print. But you never know what lawyers can do with contracts. We fought like a cat and dog for two or three consecutive days. She started calling me Mr Stump, though I'd been George to her for years. 'Mr Stump,' she would say, looking down her nose in that self-satisfied way that made you want to strangle her . . ."

"Did it?"

George Stump pulled himself up.

"You know what I mean. 'Mr Stump, I do not expect gratitude. I do not expect you to remember that your firm would have been bankrupt years ago but for me. I do not ask for special consideration. I only wish to have the courtesy which any novice being published by you might expect. You say that you will not give a publication party for the book at Kew, and raise ridiculous objections like the unwillingness of the authorities of the Royal Botanical Gardens to close their gates to the public for the occasion. Have you asked them, Mr Stump, before dismissing my modest suggestion?' And so on. I thought I should go off my rocker.

"Then a funny thing happened. Peter Davies turned her down. Said he wouldn't have her at any price. I heard this from the Secretary Alice Pink. Lillianne Bomberger became a half-starved tigress. She almost flew at me when I saw her next day. She did not tell me why, but she was no longer even a moderately sane woman. So I took advantage of it and told her that we should publish *The Flower of Death* just as we liked and when we liked and did not want any more novels from her. That was about three days before her death. I was sorry for the people round her, then."

"But you stayed here?"

"Yes. I've told you things almost like this had happened before. I believed she'd come round."

"You went to see her?"

"Certainly not. I waited."

"You didn't go to see her on her last evening alive?"

"Oh, that. Yes, but I never saw her. I went up there at about a quarter to ten, when I thought she might be a bit mellow. Pink came to the door and said she had orders not to let me in."

"Which route did you take to Trumbles?"

"I went by taxi. The inland road."

"And back the same way?"

"No. I'd dismissed the taxi. I had to walk back. Why? You surely don't suspect me of having anything to do with her death?"

"Which way did you walk back?"

"Along the sands."

"Did you meet anyone from the house?"

"No."

"Anyone you knew by sight?"

"No."

"What time did you get back to your hotel?"

"Must have been around eleven."

"Anyone see you come in?"

"I don't remember. Don't think so."

"Tell me, Mr Stump, can you remember any story by Mrs Bomberger which had any incidents or situations at all similar to those of her death?"

"Oh yes. There's an obvious one. The book was published eight years ago. Not one of her best, but its sales were well up to standard. It was called *Life Has Death for Neighbour*."

"What was the situation?"

"Some children are playing on the rocks by the seaside

and, looking into a deep rock-pool, they see a beautiful girl in it."

"Doesn't sound very similar."

"Ah, but it turns out that the girl was drowned. She had been thrown there, weighted down by a large slab of concrete."

"Who had done it?"

"Her husband, I think. Yes, her husband. The girl was a great heiress and her husband was a rotter who had been in gaol and she disowned him completely. He murdered her out of revenge."

"I understand that Lillianne Bomberger's husband has been in gaol."

"Yes."

"Has she ever seen him since?"

"Not that I know of."

"He is alive, I suppose?"

"I don't know. It's a subject she would never discuss."

"You are one of her executors? Is there any mention of Bomberger in her Will?"

"Yes. There is a sum of money for him 'if alive'.

"Is there anything else you want to tell me?"

"No. But I'd like to ask you a few questions, Deene. What do you think about this business? I mean if the woman died of an overdose of sleeping-pills why was she taken out and buried in the sand?"

"To answer that I should have to be quite sure she did die of an overdose. I don't know whether those performing the autopsy can be quite certain of that. After all, she had been in the water for some hours."

"You mean you think she may have been alive when she was buried? Why was there no sign of a struggle, then? No bruises or anything?"

"She might have been unconscious, mightn't she?"

"I suppose so. It's pretty ghastly, isn't it?"

"Murder is, Mr Stump. Whether it's a crude job with a hatchet or a subtle poisoning."

"Have you got as far as suspecting anyone yet?"

"I can't answer that question. But I would like to say this. If you have any influence with those people out at Trumbles try to get them to tell the truth. To the police or to me."

"I don't think I have much. But I'll try."

George Stump rose to leave.

"I shall be down here for a few days longer if there's anything more I can tell you."

After he had gone Carolus remained alone for nearly an hour. The case, in spite of all the obstruction made to his enquiries, was beginning very slightly to clear.

His afternoon post brought him a long envelope marked Private and Confidential, and he opened it to find the report he was awaiting on the Cribb family. He was not surprised to learn that there was a record of hereditary lunacy. Lillianne's grandfather had been certified and her sister, the mother of Gracie and Babs Stayer, had died in a mental home.

He impatiently stuffed this document into his pocket and went out to his car. He did not call for Fay or Priggley but drove alone to Trumbles.

Miss Pink opened the door.

"Good afternoon," said Carolus. "It was you I hoped to see, Miss Pink."

"Me? Oh! I don't think . . ."

"Could I see you alone for a moment? I have something for you."

He showed her the packet he had taken from Poxton on the previous night.

At first he thought she was going to faint, and caught her arm. But she rallied.

"Come in here," she said, and led him to a small sitting-room just inside the front door.

"Why did you allow yourself to be blackmailed?"

"The unpleasantness . . ." tried Miss Pink.

"What unpleasantness? There couldn't be any more.

You'd had everything from police enquiries to newspaper reports."

"It all seemed . . . he said he could make it unpleasant . . ."

"Why? What did he know?"

"Please don't question me, Mr Deene. I'm far from well."

"He must have known something that you wanted to keep hidden. What was it?"

"Nothing. Nothing. Do the police know about these?"

"Not yet."

"Oh dear, I don't know what to say. . . . It's all so . . . How did you get these? Is he angry?"

"Never mind. Now for God's sake, woman, speak the truth. You wouldn't have got together five hundred pounds and handed it over to that wretched man unless you had something serious to hide. What was it?"

"Didn't he tell you?" In her desperation Alice Pink had prodded the weakest point of Carolus.

"I want to hear from you."

"Then he *didn't* tell you! Don't question me any more, Mr Deene. There is nothing to tell you." A sort of faded triumph crept into her voice. "Nothing at all."

Carolus knew that for the moment at least he was beaten.

"There is one other thing," he said quietly. "Did you ever meet Mrs Bomberger's husband?"

Alice Pink took a moment to focus.

"No. I never actually met him."

"Do you know whether he's alive?"

"Oh yes, I think so. Mrs Bomberger wrote to him some time ago."

"What did she say?"

"She did not dictate the letter. She wrote it herself and addressed the envelope."

"But you saw it?"

"Well, quite by chance. I was looking for her spectacles. . . ."

"What was the address?"

"I don't know exactly. The letter was addressed to Otto Bomberger in Brighton."

"That is the only time?"

"Yes. But I *have* fancied—I don't know why; perhaps it was something Mrs Bomberger said—that he had cropped up again lately. And a few days before her death—that is *nothing* but conjecture, Mr Deene—she instructed me to draw five hundred pounds from her bank in one pound notes."

"You have no idea what her purpose was?"

"None."

"What became of them?"

Miss Pink was silent.

"It's pretty obvious, isn't it? You used them to square this miserable blackmailer. Well, that's nothing to do with me. I'm only interested in murder."

Carolus looked sadly at the frightened and fussy creature, but decided that it was useless to persuade her again to tell him the truth.

12

Two days later, as Carolus was passing down Sandringham Terrace, the door of Number Thirty-Seven opened and he saw Mrs Plum beckoning to him vigorously.

"Come in quick and shut the door before anyone sees you, though goodness knows there's enough peeping and prying in this street. I once told her, where you're living, that she needn't think I couldn't see her behind the lace curtains. Well, I thought it would come. They give me my cards this morning. Don't want me up there any more. And I don't wonder at it, with what's going on."

She paused for breath and Carolus waited patiently.

"Come in the front room a minute, where no one's going to hear, because if anyone was to get to know some of the things I've seen I wouldn't answer for it. It's like the haunted house in the fairground, you never know what you're going to come on next, and I'm glad to have got away alive because it was turning me into nothing but a mass of nerves. Time and time I've said I didn't mean to go back and I wish I hadn't months ago so's I wouldn't have heard all I have. Sometimes when I walked out of that gate my legs were wobbling like jellies and I didn't know how I should ever get to the bus-stop."

"What particular thing . . ."

"Particular thing? It was no good being particular with murders going on and them having the hystericals and that. But these last two days it has been that Pink. Do you know what she did yesterday? It gives me the shudders when I think about it. She tried to do for herself."

"Suicide, you mean?"

Mrs Plum gave her violent mandarin nod.

"That's what it was, unless I'm very much mistaken. She was upset all the morning and I could see she'd been crying, her eyes were that red and swollen. I thought, and well she might cry; so might anyone if they lived in that place and knew what she knows with people being murdered and buried and that. She's been upset for a long time, but yesterday morning it came to a pitch. Then no sooner was dinner over—and I don't believe she ate a thing—she went up to her room and was on the typewriter for a bit, because I could hear her when I went past to the linen cupboard.

"Then she came down with her hat on and marched into the room where Gracie and Babs were. 'I'm going to end it,' she said. 'Now. This afternoon.' 'Don't be silly, Alice,' said one of them. 'Everything's going to be all right.' 'It's not. It's not. I tell you he knows.' 'Keep calm now,' said Babs. 'It's never as bad as it seems. You weren't to know.' 'I didn't know!' So they went on, she saying she was going to end it all and they telling her to keep quiet. After that she flung out of the house.

"Well, I thought, that'll be a nice thing if she goes and does for herself and we have two corpses on our hands. It sent cold shivers up and down my spine to think of it. I thought I should go off into convulsions. But no, an hour later she was back, looking quite different. Cool as a cucumber, she was, as though she'd forgotten all her troubles. Yes, I thought, you can look as though you hadn't a care in the world, but what about the murder that's still hanging over us like a nightmare? But I didn't say anything—well, it wasn't my place to. I was pleased to see the poor thing look a little better.

"She went upstairs to her room, and in a few minutes she was tearing down again shouting out as though there was someone after her with a carving-knife. It turned me to a lump of ice to hear her; I really thought the end of the world had come. 'Where's my letter?' she says to me. 'What letter, Miss Pink?' I asked, because I had no idea what she was talking about. 'The letter I left on the type-writer,' she said, and her eyes were wild like anybody who's escaped from a lunatic asylum. 'I don't know, I'm sure,' I said. 'I haven't seen any letter nor yet been into your room nor touched your typewriter. And may I drop dead if I'd do any such thing.' 'Then who has?' she asks. 'I'm sure I don't know,' I said. 'I've got my work to think of without trapezing about looking for letters.' 'Someone has!' she said, and went off to find Gracie and Babs. Nice thing, wasn't it? I suppose what she'd done was to type out fare-well for ever, then think better of it and come back to find someone had took her dying words off the typewriter for a joke, as you might say.

"I only heard one bit more before I came away yesterday —that was when the door was open for a minute while they was having tea. I just caught Miss Pink say something like: 'I shall. I shall. I've been foolish. Whatever happens can't be worse than this.' I may not have it quite right, but that's what it sounded like. But I didn't like it. It made me feel a bit squeamy. Seemed as though I'd gone hollow in-side. Then there was the other thing."

This time Carolus felt a question might help.

"What other thing?"

"Well, about that Graveston. The way he speaks to them all. Good as you are, if you know what I mean. No 'Miss' and 'Ma'am' or anything—talking to all three of them and Ron Cribb and his wife as though they were old friends. I heard him say to Gracie, 'What you better do is to tell her . . .' and so on. It sounded so funny in that deep voice of his. It was almost as though it was his house now and Gracie and them no more than what they always was. It upset me, really it did. I thought, whatever does this mean, because whatever it is it's not right for him to be talking like that. He's never done it before, ever since I've worked there, anyway. Gave me a nasty taste, like some-thing that's Gone Off. But there you are. It was only part of all the rest, and I'll be thankful not to tread the threshold of that house ever again. It was bad enough when Mrs Bomberger was alive and she and that Mr Stump shouting at one another like two mad bulls."

"Really?"

"He was the only one who seemed able to stand up to her —well, towards the end he did; in the old days he was worse than any of them, running round trying to please her. It was as though he saw it coming. The last few times he was there he got quite uppish and answered her back as good as she gave. She turned round to him one day and said, 'You'll never get another book of mine, Mr Stump.' So he turned round and said, 'I wouldn't take another if you offered it me.' At that she turned round to him white as a sheet and said, 'You insulting little stationer,' she said. I remember the very words, because I wondered whatever she meant. He turned round quietly when she said that and told her, 'I should be proud to be a stationer even if it was true,' he said; 'what I should be ashamed to have done is to have spent my whole life feebly imitating better writers.' Then I thought she really would go up in a sheet of flames. She turned round and shouted, 'Get out of my house! Get out, and don't ever try to return!' It was enough to make anyone feel bad, those two shouting at one another all the insults they could think of, though after that Mr Stump did go off and we had a few minutes' peace and quiet."

"It's very kind of you to trouble to tell me all that, Mrs Plum."

"Oh, I had to. I couldn't sleep at night for thinking about it. I thought, if I don't tell someone this I shall turn into I don't know what. I mean it's enough to give anyone the jim-jams when you come to think of it. D'you think that Alice Pink will have another go at doing for herself?"

"I think the situation is very dangerous."

"And you're right! I don't know whatever made me take it in the first place. Oh, and Mr Primmley's got something he wants to tell you. He's the gardener up there. He's married to my husband's cousin and got ever such a bonny little girl."

"How can I get hold of him?"

"Well, without you go up there and see him at his cottage, I don't know. I tell you what though: he's on the Gardeners' and Allotment-Holders' Committee, and they meet every Thursday at the Feathers, so you could see him tonight if you was to go down there about eight. He doesn't seem much bothered by what's gone on up at the house, I must say, but then he always kept himself to himself. You tell him I told you to ask for him, and he'll tell you what he told me he wanted to tell you."

Carolus was wondering when he would be allowed to leave, and the same problem seemed to be worrying Mrs Plum.

"If you go marching out of the front door, one of them's bound to see you," she said.

"Does it matter much now that you're no longer working up there?"

"Well, I don't want them to know my business, specially when it's anything like this. One of them's bound to tell *her*, where you're living, when she comes back and that would never do. Still, I don't see much help for it, I must say, so you better go as quick as you can and turn down the road first like you did before."

Carolus obeyed, wondering once more whether he would ever hear the name of 'her, where you're living', since in all the references to his landlady she had never been given more than a pronoun. He decided he would not ask, for surely he had plenty of questions to put without this one.

A heavy sea-mist came up that evening and enveloped the town. It was so thick that at eight o'clock, when Carolus set out for the pub called the Prince of Wales Feathers, which he had learned was the one designated by Mrs Plum, he left his car and went on foot.

A burly landlord, giving him a fair measure of whisky, said that yes, he knew Tom Primmley. He was up in the club-room at the moment with the rest of the committee, but they usually broke up about now, and he'd catch him coming down.

"Nasty business that where he works, isn't it? You couldn't ask for a more generous lady than Mrs Bomberger," said the publican.

Carolus was interested in this, positively the first words he had heard in praise of the dead woman.

"In what way, generous?" he asked.

"She'd done a lot for the town. No one asking her for a subscription was ever turned away. Mind you, I'm not saying she didn't like her name on the list and in the paper and that, but I reckon she was entitled to it. Even the clergy only had to go to her."

"You'd say she was popular in Blessington?"

"She wasn't known much personally. But when it came to giving she was the first. Ah, here's Tom. Tom, this gentleman's waiting to speak to you."

Primmley was a merry little man with thick grey hair and a healthy red face. He looked enquiringly at Carolus.

"Mrs Plum told me I should find you here," Carolus explained. "I hear you have something to tell me. My name's Deene and I'm trying to find out the truth about Mrs Bomberger's death."

Sitting behind a pint of ale in a corner of the bar, Primmley talked with a natural chuckle running among his words.

"It's not really much, sir, but as I'd told it to the police I thought I might as well tell it to you. Fair's fair, isn't it? I've read enough detective novels to know that it isn't always easy for anyone like you to get at the truth."

"Thank you."

"It's like this. I never had much to do with them up at the house. My wife and I have got our cottage and a little girl, with another expected. Mrs Bomberger used to leave me alone generally, though she could be very sarcastic about the garden sometimes. 'Oh, Primmley,' she would say in that nasty, pleased-with-herself way of hers, 'I'm quite aware that I mustn't expect to see miracles, but in view of the very large sum I spent on plants and seeds at your request I do think I might sometimes have a little colour about the place. I know that people write very poetically about the bare earth, but it does grow somewhat monotonous.' And that with my dahlias ablaze and winning every prize at the show and the chrysanths coming along lovely. Still, it never worried me. You see, sir, when you work in a garden it's as though it was your own and you've no one really to please but yourself. However, that's not what you want to know."

"Please go on."

"Right up to the last the wife and I never thought of anything. She'd heard a few bits here and there from Mrs Plum, whose late husband was a distant relative of hers, but nothing out of the usual. Nor on the last day there wasn't. I did my work and didn't see anything much of them. It was during the night."

"Yes?"

"The wife's a very light sleeper. Any little thing will wake her, and she has a job to get off again. That night I felt her shaking me. I wasn't best pleased about that, but I could see she was a bit upset. 'Whatever's the matter?' I asked. 'Oh, Tom, you've left the light on in your potting-shed,' she told me. 'I woke just now and went to look out of the window.' I asked what had woken her, but she didn't rightly know. She said she thought she'd heard someone talking over there, but she couldn't be sure whether it wasn't in her sleep. 'Anyway, I got up and looked out,' she said, 'and saw the light in your shed. However did you come to leave it on?' 'I didn't,' I said flat, because I wanted to get back to sleep. 'I didn't do any such thing. I haven't been in the potting-shed since five o'clock when I put my tools away, and there was plenty of light then. Besides, I never leave it on.' 'Well, it's on now,' she said, and I got up to look. When I reached the window the wife was quite

114

excited. 'Someone's put it out!' she said. 'I saw it on as plain as anything just now. Someone must have seen it and put it out.'

"It was a funny thing, because my wife's a sensible woman. She's a good bit younger than me, but I've never known her imagine things like that. 'All right,' I said, 'I'll go across and see what it's all about.' 'You'll do no such thing,' she said; 'waking the child and everything. You go back to bed.' I wish I had gone now. I might have had something worth telling. But when it all came out what had happened in the night the wife was right, of course. 'Didn't I tell you?' she said almost before we heard the news. 'You might have got your throat cut.' That's what she said. But then women are always right, aren't they, sir?"

Fortified with another pint, Tom Primmley prepared to answer questions.

"What time did this happen?" Carolus asked.

"The police asked me that. But it's just what I can't tell you. It was well on in the night, I'm sure of that, but it was before any sign of morning. I never thought to look at my watch."

"When you went over to your potting-shed did you find anything out of place?"

"Not to be certain of, I didn't. I never lock it; you don't need to round here and it's right near the house. The door was shut as usual. Everything seemed just as I left it, unless it was . . ."

"Yes?"

"I can't be sure of this, but I did think that perhaps the big tools in the corner had been interfered with. I told the police that, and they took them all away to look for finger prints. The wife heard afterwards that on one spade they'd found Graveston's prints and questioned him about it. But Graveston told them he'd borrowed that spade from me a day or two before to dig up where a drain was blocked outside the kitchen window."

"That was true, was it?"

"Quite true. I don't get on too well with Graveston, who's a sign-the-pledge chapel-goer, but it's true enough he borrowed a spade, and I don't think I've used it since. Anything else you want to know?"

"No. But if you do see anything up at Trumbles that strikes you as odd you might let me know. Mrs Plum knows where I live."

"I will, sir. Mrs Bomberger left me a bit of money, but I don't like to take it till this is all cleared up."

"How are you going to get back in this mist?" asked Carolus.

"Oh, that's all right, sir. I know the way like the back of my hand. I've got my old bicycle. I shall go round by the road."

As Carolus groped his way to Wee Hoosie he was glad that he had no need to visit Trumbles that evening.

13

NEXT morning Carolus was awakened by Mrs Stick. The little woman sounded perturbed.

"Miss Fay's here," she said, "and wants to see you at once. Says it's important."

"Tell her I'll be down in a minute."

Carolus dressed and found Fay bolt upright on one of his horsehair chairs.

"Oh, Carolus, it's really rather awful. Pink—you know, Alice Pink the Secretary who looks rather like a *bat*. I don't mean a vampire, just an ordinary domestic bat—well, she has disappeared."

"I shan't hurry you, my dear Fay, or ask you questions, because I realize that you'll tell me all you know in good time if you're allowed your measure of chaos."

"You know I can never get things straight, as people say, but this really does seem a bit upsetting. I mean the poor creature's been in such a tizzy for weeks that anything may have happened. For years, really. Bomberger was a sort of huge Kali to her. She just walked out of the house last night, it seems, and hasn't come back. It wasn't so unusual for her to go out at night—just lately she's been behaving like somebody in *Wuthering Heights* or something. But it is unusual for her not to come back."

"I see that," smiled Carolus.

"Oh, shut up! You know what I mean. I was in my bath this morning when Babs phoned and told me. I asked if she wanted me to tell you, but she didn't seem to know. Pink's not been more odd than usual during the last few days; she is, of course, psychopathic. The two girls are quite worried about it. They're alone in the house with that fearful Graveston."

"Have they told the police?"

"They hadn't when they phoned me. I begged them to at once. I hope they will. It seems Pink took no baggage with her, which makes it all a bit sinister. Of course she may have escaped on impulse, but if she *meant* to come back it looks as though she has had it."

"When she went for these nocturnal walks which way did she take?"

"According to Babs, what Pink has taken to doing in the evening is to put together for herself a few sandwiches and march off at about eight, staying out till ten or eleven. She didn't like having her evening meal with them, apparently. They even thought at first that she was meeting someone, but Graveston saw her quite alone in the shelter at the top of the cliff, eating her sandwiches and, according to him, 'swallowing from a flask' which he suspected to contain alcohol. She has rather taken to a drop of gin since Bomberger's death, it seems."

"Was that the route she took last night?"

"They don't know. It was misty, you remember, one of those heavy sea-mists which last a few hours and come and go with the moon. No one saw her leave, but they realized she had gone at about eight-thirty and got very worried. In fact Babs went off to try to find her, shouting her name all over the place without result. When she got back she sent Graveston, and as Primmley came in about that time she sent him. The Cribbs were spending the evening at Trumbles, and it seems they went out and looked for her, too. Gracie and Babs couldn't bear to think of that poor thing wandering about in the mist, and stayed up till all the search-parties were back with nothing to report. They went to bed at last hoping that she would come in during the night, but this morning, when Babs went to Pink's room, she found that the bed hadn't been slept in, and came down to phone me."

"I suppose I shall have to go out there," said Carolus. "I didn't want to again. They lie so."

"Poor things! What do you expect them to do? Everyone lies over a thing like this."

"Yes. Pink did certainly. All right, let me eat something and we'll go."

Mrs Stick brought in coffee and rolls, and Carolus munched quickly while Fay rattled on.

"I do think you might have solved the thing before this, Carolus. That wretched Pink wandering about somewhere . . ."

"If she's still alive."

"Why not? I shouldn't have thought there was anything suicidal about her. A nervous *string* of a woman like that is usually as tough as they come in a crisis. You don't think she has been murdered, do you?"

"I think it's possible."

"I suppose she's going to be found with her head out of the sand, now. Why can't you stop this thing, Carolus? You're supposed to be such an ace. If there's a murderer here you ought to have had him or her days ago, and if there isn't you should have said so and stopped those women worrying."

"What about the cousin and his wife?"

"Ron and Gloria? They simply say they could not find Pink or get an answer to their calls."

"And Graveston?"

"Babs didn't mention him."

"Let's get out there and hear some more lies," said Carolus.

"Don't be too hard on those two women, Carolus. They've had years of hell with Bomberger and a bad time since her death. They're pretty near breaking-point. I know them."

They reached Trumbles at about ten o'clock and were admitted by Gracie.

"No word?" asked Fay.

Gracie shook her head. "I'm afraid . . ."

Carolus tried in the interview that followed to treat the two sisters with more gentleness than on previous occasions. He started by questions about Miss Pink's family.

"I believe she had a sister," said Babs, "who is Matron of a hospital or boys' school. 'My sister, the Matron,' was mentioned from time to time. No one else."

"Where was her home?"

"We've never quite known. There was talk of 'my old home in Hampshire' and I don't know why but I have an idea that her father was a solicitor. She may have said so."

"Do you think we could find the sister's name and address among Miss Pink's papers?"

Watching closely, Carolus thought that the sisters narrowly avoided exchanging glances.

"I shouldn't think so. She had practically no personal papers."

"We could try," said Carolus.

Babs rose quickly.

"I'll run up and look at once," she said. Before there could be any argument she left the room.

"Have you yet informed the police?" Carolus asked Gracie.

"No. Must we? It is so hateful to have them asking questions."

"Of course you must. I suggest you do so immediately."

"Babs said . . ."

"Miss Stayer, this is a serious and urgent matter. Fay, call the police at once."

There was a general hesitation.

"I suppose you had better," said Gracie at last. "There's a phone over there. Oh dear, I shall be glad when all this is over."

While Fay was still talking, Babs returned.

"I've found it," she said. "Miss Ethel Pink, St Mervyn's Preparatory School, Porthpillo, near Penzance. It was on a list of addresses in a drawer of her table."

Carolus took the phone when Fay had finished and began

to dictate. "*Your sister Alice Pink worried by recent unexplained death of employer Lillianne Bomberger went out last evening not returned Stop. Possibly on her way to you Stop. Please wire whether other relatives or suggestions where might go. Stop. Police informed and all steps taken.*

"Now tell me about yesterday," he invited Gracie and Babs Stayer.

It was Babs who answered.

"She seemed rather depressed all day, but then she has been depressed lately. I suppose we all have. But she did not say anything unusual. She has formed some rather odd habits since my aunt's death."

"Such as?"

"Locking herself up in her room for long periods. And these evening walks on the cliff."

"Always on the cliff?"

"We don't know. The only time she has been seen was when Graveston came on her in that little shelter they have made right at the highest point between here and Blessington. She never ate much in the house, but she used to take sandwiches with her at night. It was rather peculiar, you will own."

"Did she drink?"

"Never, when my aunt was alive. At least, not so far as anyone knew. But we have been rather surprised lately. She does like a nip. We caught her pouring herself out a snorter one morning. Graveston says she had a flask with her the other night."

"Was it her flask?"

"I think it was Aunt Lillianne's. She had a little silver one which hasn't been seen lately."

"You think Miss Pink had it last night?"

"Probably. Actually, I never thought she would go out last night. There was a sea-mist all round us here. She went to her room at about seven and didn't appear again. We prepared a scratch meal for ourselves and Ron and Gloria, who had come over. We called her when it was ready, but there was no reply. Then we rather panic'd, I'm afraid. I felt she ought not to be wandering about alone and went out to try and find her."

"Which way did you go?" asked Carolus.

"Well, actually I didn't go very far. It was a bit tricky last night, and I had an idea she had gone up on the cliffs. I shouted for her and started to climb a little way, but I'm afraid gave it up then."

"How long do you think you were gone?"

"I don't know. I daresay about twenty minutes."

"Did it seem like that to you?" Carolus asked Gracie.

"Babs was much longer. She's braver than she would have you think. I wouldn't have gone out alone in that mist for anything. I'm sure she hunted everywhere."

"Yes?"

"And even then she wouldn't rest. She sent Graveston and Primmley out to look for Miss Pink. Then she suggested to Ron that he might have a look in the other direction, and he and Gloria went out. I didn't like going to bed. Nor did Babs. And first thing this morning Babs went to her room and found she hadn't been in all night."

"Has anyone been over the cliff footpath today to see whether . . ."

"We sent Graveston up about half an hour ago. He should be back any minute."

"There has never been any suggestion of suicide on her part?"

This was the first question which seemed to make the two sisters uncomfortable.

"I've always rather wondered," said Babs at last. "But more in my aunt's time than now. She seemed to me rather the type."

"She has never said anything to make you anticipate this?"

"No. In moments of great stress she would talk about 'ending it all', as people do."

"Has she had one of those moments of great stress lately?"

Babs seemed strangely tense and thoughtful during these questions.

"I believe she had the other day. But . . ."

"Which day?"

"I think it was the day before yesterday. But it was nothing extraordinary. Just Alice Pink getting excited. None of us thought of taking it seriously."

Carolus remained silent for a moment. Then, looking at Babs, he asked if he might have a word with Mrs Plum.

"We've had to get rid of her," said Babs. "She was really too much. She got such a kick out of all this that she became unbearable. She would run about the house staring at one and having what she called the creeps or the shudders at everything. We decided we would rather do the work ourselves."

Carolus nodded. The explanation was reasonable.

"I think," he said, "I'll leave you before the police get here. Fay, would you drive the car back? I want to go by the footpath over the cliffs."

It was a cloudy morning with a damp breeze, and as he began to climb up the fairly steep hillside Carolus saw very few holiday-makers. The 'footpath' was about six feet wide and was of asphalt. There was a certain amount of litter visible in spite of the receptacles placed for it.

But the benevolent Borough Council which had made this little footpath an extension of the town promenade had not yet gone to the expense of lighting it, so that no ugly light-standards marred the hillside.

A tall figure advanced towards him, and he recognized Graveston.

"I've just come from the house," Carolus told him. "I heard that I should meet you."

"Yes. I have been as far as the shelter to which Miss Pink usually went. . . ."

"Usually?"

For the first time Graveston was clearly discomforted.

"That is . . . she is known to have gone. . . ."

"*How* is she known to have gone?" snapped Carolus, at last finding a gap in defences.

"I myself have seen her . . ."

"How often?"

"I could not say. On several occasions. She went up there in the evening."

"You followed her?"

"I found my way was hers. I had meetings to attend in Blessington."

"And this morning?"

"The ladies of the house instructed me to come and see if . . . if there were any sign of Miss Pink."

"Was there?"

"None that I could see. She was certainly not in the shelter."

"You have found nothing at all to make you think she came this way?"

"Nothing."

With a curt nod Carolus walked on. He found the climb quite a stiff one, and was not surprised that there had been difficulty in wheeling a bath-chair here containing the heavy frame of Lillianne Bomberger.

From the crest he could see the shelter and half a mile farther on the Coast Guards' station, which looked from here almost on the outskirts of Blessington. He walked fast, not bothering to examine oddments of litter in his way. It took him about eight minutes to reach the shelter, and here he stopped.

It was built of metal, with glass divisions, the same structure as one finds in any coastal town in England, but it looked rather forlorn alone here on the hill. It stood perhaps fifty yards from the edge of the cliff on ground which sloped slightly downwards towards the sea.

Carolus made a careful examination of its interior, but found no object to appropriate and apparently nothing to occupy his particular attention. Then he started walking very slowly, his eyes downcast, towards the cliff's edge.

The grass was short and dry and there were dried rabbit and sheep droppings, but nothing which made Carolus pause long. When he drew near to the cliff's edge he stopped and looked about him.

At first he thought that there was no one in sight. Then back in the direction of Trumbles he saw a tall, dark figure standing. He recognized, or believed that he recognized, Graveston. He was at least half a mile away and there was no one nearer.

Now Carolus faced an inward combat which had gone on in him at intervals all his life and particularly during his years in a parachute regiment during the war. He feared heights. It was in order to gain the victory in that fearful internal struggle that he had joined a parachute regiment, and no one had ever suspected that he was fighting against himself in doing so.

He knew from his observation from the sands below that the cliff here was at its highest. It was not a sheer and clean-cut cliff like that of Beachy Head but a broken drop with ledges and even some vegetation on its surface. To go over its edge would almost certainly mean to reach the foot of it. The fall might be broken, but there was little chance of any object being caught on the way down.

Now Carolus lay flat on the ground and slowly crawled towards the edge. In this way he could avoid any danger from vertigo, from which at heights, and increasingly since the war, he suffered.

When he reached the edge and peered over he saw what by now he almost expected to see. About half-way down the cliff, on a jagged shelf of rock, was all that remained of Alice Pink. Carolus did not wait to observe the gruesome details, but he saw enough to know, without any doubt at all, that she was dead.

He drew back from the edge, crawled backward like a

snake and lay for a moment quite still looking down at the clean green turf. Then he vomited.

It was ten minutes before Carolus was back on the asphalt path and on his way to Blessington. He recovered quickly in the fresh, breezy air.

It took him half an hour to reach his temporary home, and he was by no means pleased to find Priggley waiting for him. He was about to dismiss him when Priggley said, "Where on earth have you been? I've got a message for you. I came here at the crack of dawn, but you had already gone out."

"What's the message?" said Carolus curtly.

"It's from Alice Pink, the secretary. She rang up yesterday evening, thinking you were still at the hotel."

"Why didn't you come and tell me at once?"

"I came round, but you weren't in. If you *will* live in a place without a telephone! And anyway it didn't seem urgent. She wants you to see her today—not out at Trumbles, but here in the town. She's coming in at three o'clock this afternoon, when her absence there won't be noticed. She has decided to tell you everything. She will wait for you in the Lounge of the Royal Hydro."

"She won't," said Carolus. "She's dead."

14

CAROLUS went straight to the police station and explained to the desk sergeant that he wanted to see the CID officer in charge of the Bomberger case.

The desk sergeant, like many English policemen, had been as long in the military as in the civil police and had the same unsure, overbearing manner as a CMP corporal who has detected an officer in an offence.

"Why? Have you got some information to give?" he asked sharply.

"I shouldn't have come here to pass the time of day," said Carolus.

"If you have any information it's your duty . . ."

"I asked if the officer in charge of the case was in," said Carolus quietly. He saw the approach of one of those wearisome arguments with which policemen everywhere bolster up their self-importance. "Would you be kind enough to tell me?"

There was an exchange of hostile looks, after which the desk sergeant said, "No. He's not back yet."

"You're expecting him?"

"He should be here."

"Then I'll wait."

Carolus opened a newspaper and the desk sergeant turned his attention to his papers, and five minutes passed in silence. Then someone entered behind Carolus and went to an inner door. The desk sergeant nodded to a policeman, who followed the man in and came back to invite Carolus to the CID office.

Detective Inspector Whibley was a big, jovial man, rather consciously in what is called the prime of life. His smile was too ready, his handshake too forceful, his manner altogether too friendly for Carolus in his present mood.

"Sit down, Mr Deene. I know all about you, and I'm glad you've come to see me. I heard you were interesting yourself in the Bomberger case and expected we should meet sooner or later."

"I have something to report," said Carolus.

"Oh yes? Have a cigarette, will you? It's an interesting case, as I expect you've found. What have you to report, Mr Deene?"

"A corpse," said Carolus.

"Oh, ho!" smiled the Inspector. "A corpse, eh? Do you know whose?"

"Yes. Alice Pink's."

The detective seemed for the first time to take something seriously.

"Her disappearance was reported this morning," he said.

"You'll find her lying about half-way down the cliffs between here and Trumbles Bay. If you go as far as the shelter and look down the cliff in front of that you can see what's left of her."

"Badly disfigured?"

"Disfigured? Oh hell! You go and see for yourself."

"I will, Mr Deene. How did you come to discover this?"

"Reasoning, more or less."

"You don't mean you anticipated it?"

"No. Not that. But I saw the possibility. When she disappeared I asked what her recent habits were, and found one of them was to walk up to that shelter in the evening. There was a certain amount of accidental or deliberate lying about that, by the way, Babs Stayer saying that Graveston had seen her there *once*, Graveston saying it was on a number of occasions. Anyway, I knew she went there, so I walked up this morning, looked over the edge and saw her body."

"Do you think it was suicide, Mr Deene?"

"I have no opinion."

"You don't wish to say any more?"

"If you are open to a suggestion, Detective Inspector . . ."

"Certainly, Mr Deene. Cer-tainly. We're always open to suggestions. We're not the hidebound fools you private investigators seem to think."

"Then I suggest that when you have recovered the body of Alice Pink you have an autopsy in . . ."

"Of course we shall. But in these cases it's seldom much use. How can any doctor say whether a wound was received before the fall or during it? The limbs will be damaged, anyway."

"I wasn't thinking of the limbs, so much as the intestines."

"Good gracious, Mr Deene. You surprise me. From what you say I shouldn't have thought we had to look farther for the cause of death than the fall down the cliff-side."

"It is merely a suggestion."

"I'll bear it in mind, Mr Deene, and should there be any result I will see that you hear of it. After all"—the Detective Inspector beamed—"after all, we owe you our prompt discovery of the cadaver, don't we?"

"Perhaps you feel like throwing me a few more bits of information."

"Such as?"

"Oh, never mind." Carolus knew that he would hear nothing which the police regarded as important.

"I'll tell you one thing," said the detective, with a confiding smile. "One thing that you may not know, that is. Bomberger was in the town at the time of his wife's death."

Carolus said, "I had suspected it, but I'm grateful to you for telling me. Where can he be found?"

"Lives in Brighton. You can find him at a pub called the Green Star."

"Under his own name?"

"No. White."

He knew from the detective's seeming generosity that not the slightest suspicion, in the police mind, attached to Bomberger.

"I'd better tell you something, too," he said. "Though if you don't know this you ought to. You have better means of discovering it than I have. There is inherited lunacy in the Cribb family."

"I didn't know that, Mr Deene. But I do not think it very significant, since the only members of the family with whom we have to deal are certainly sane people."

"That is so."

"Now I must go out and find this unfortunate woman's corpse. Still recognizable, I suppose?"

"Just," said Carolus and left.

He managed to eat a quick lunch which Mrs Stick had ready for him, but he was restless and did not mean to remain more than a few minutes in the stuffy, crowded atmosphere of Wee Hoosie. Stick, using the carpenter's tools which he dearly loved, had managed to unscrew the windows and let in a little air, but an age of unventilated living had made the house a tomb. Or so it seemed to Carolus that afternoon.

He was going out of the door when he saw approaching a fine, masterful woman with unnaturally auburn hair and a determined chin.

"Mr Deene? My name is Ethel Pink."

"But . . ."

"There is nothing miraculous in my appearance," she admitted in a firm voice. "Miss Stayer told me of your telegram. It has crossed me, as it were. I was coming to see Alice in any case. At her urgent request. Fortunately the school holidays made possible my absence from St Mervyn's."

"Come in," said Carolus. "Miss Stayer sent you to me?"

"She suggested that you might be able to tell me something about my sister's sudden disappearance."

"Unhappily I can, Miss Pink. Your sister is dead."

The Matron of St Mervyn's looked at Carolus steadily, and it was impossible to guess her emotions.

"Murdered?" she said at last.

"Possibly."

"It can't have been suicide."

"I don't know."

"Where was she found?"

"Half-way down the highest cliffs near here."

"Pushed over?"

"The body hasn't yet been recovered. The police have that in hand."

"Bound to be publicity, I suppose? Name Pink and that?"

"I'm afraid so."

"Bad for the school."

Carolus looked rather bitterly at Ethel Pink.

"You should meet Mr Gorringer," he said. "You two would get on wonderfully well. Now I should like to ask you a few questions, if I may. Had your sister any tendency to suicide?"

"None. As a girl she was more frivolous than I, but later learnt a sense of responsibility. I have no doubt she was an excellent secretary."

"When did you see her last?"

"A year ago. We spent a week together in London. Three theatres and the Academy."

"Did she discuss her employer then?"

"Frequently. She wished to leave Mrs Bomberger."

"Why didn't she?"

"A mystery. When it came to it she wouldn't. A complete mystery."

"She was well paid?"

"I believe so. That was not the reason, however. Alice had means of her own," said Ethel Pink surprisingly.

"Then why?"

"I never knew the late Mrs Bomberger, but I gather she

had considerable force of character. Alice had none. None."

"I see."

"All our lives she has had to lean on me. Fortunately my character and constitution have enabled me to supply the necessary drive."

Carolus nodded in complete agreement.

"You think she stayed with Mrs Bomberger because she was too weak to leave her?"

"Exactly. She was putty, Mr Deene. Putty. Which makes her death the more extraordinary. My sister would not have had the courage for suicide. Quite out of the question."

"You may well be right."

"She was certainly murdered. No doubt of it. I can supply the explanation."

"Really?"

"Yes. She knew too much. That's what caused her to be liquidated. *She knew too much.*"

"What evidence have you for that?"

"Her last letter. Received two days ago. Leaves not a doubt of it."

"May I see it?"

"Of course. I have no secrets. Except one," she added as a grim afterthought.

"That?" asked Carolus, fascinated.

"How to deal with the staff at St Mervyn's. Believe me, that's a secret I've had to learn. It's a case of the survival of the fittest at St Mervyn's."

"It must be a very interesting school."

"It is. Here's the letter. Read it for yourself. You'll see that it leaves no room for doubt."

Carolus read:

Dear Ethel,

　　　I am writing this under a great stress and I hope you will appreciate the seriousness of it, as I badly need your advice and if possible your presence here. Do you think you could manage to come as soon as possible? It would be a great relief to me if you could. Of course I realize that your responsibilities and obligations at St Mervyn's are *paramount*, but this is a case of life and death.

You have read in the paper, I expect, of the death of Mrs Bomberger and how her body was found buried in the sand. Unfortunately I know something of the circumstances which I cannot repeat, for reasons which I will explain to you when you come (as I hope you will). The police have questioned me *rigorously*, and that is a very disagreeable experience. Also a private detective named Carolus Deene. I am sorely tempted to tell him what I know and have done with it, but there are reasons why this would be a foolish step to take.

I think you will realize the seriousness of my position when I say that *it was I who gave Mrs Bomberger her sleeping-pills that night*. I really do not know what to do for the best and have recently come near to the sin of self-destruction.

If we could only have a good talk about it, as we used to talk in our bedroom at Basingstoke (remember?), I should feel better and perhaps you might see a way out of this difficult situation. But you have so often said that St Mervyn's comes first that I wonder whether you will be able to come in answer to this urgent appeal.

I will write no more now, only hoping that you will come.

Your affectionate sister,

Alice.

"I don't quite see how this letter is evidence that your sister knew too much, as you put it. It seems to me to involve only herself."

Ethel Pink looked at Carolus in a manner usually reserved for members of the staff at St Mervyn's who had encroached on her province.

"You don't? My dear man, it's obvious. 'I know something of the circumstances which I cannot repeat', she says."

133

"It may be something which only implicates herself."

"Nonsense! It's as plain as a pikestaff. The poor girl knew too much and has suffered for it."

"She admits to having administered the pills from which, as far as we know, Mrs Bomberger died."

"Alice could never administer anything, least of all a large and busy school. But let that pass. What are you doing about her death?"

"I have reported it to the police. They have probably recovered the body by now and will require you to identify it."

See how you like that, Carolus could not help thinking.

Ethel Pink nodded. "It will be my duty," she said. "I meant what are you doing about her murderer? When will he be discovered?"

"I do not know yet that she was murdered."

"I shall stay here till you have cleared the matter up!" threatened Miss Pink.

"That is for you to decide, of course."

"I shall see the police myself and tell them my sister was murdered."

"Yes. Do that."

"I understand you're a schoolmaster?"

"I am. Yes."

"Tssssttt!" said Miss Pink contemptuously, and left after the briefest nod of leave-taking.

This time Carolus made no attempt to go out, but sat down in the least uncomfortable of the chairs as though, like a Yogi, he could think deeply and to order. He remained nearly an hour there and was disturbed only by the entrance of Priggley.

"What do you want?" he asked wearily.

"Nothing, really. It's just that I'm getting a bit worried about this case, sir. You really are slipping, you know."

Carolus did not reply.

"For instance, do you deny that you could have prevented the death of Alice Pink?"

"I don't see how."

"Are you anywhere near a solution?"

"If you want me to be really explicit, I am and I'm not. It's all terribly circumstantial. There's nothing for me or the police to get our teeth into."

"I see that. But if these two women were murdered it does make you look a bit slow, to say the least of it."

"I know. I don't pretend to be happy about this case."

"It looked like a pretty frolic to start with, didn't it? I mean no one could miss the Bomberger."

"Apparently not."

"Oh, by the way, I've got something to tell you. That squint-eyed character is back. Or else he never left the town. I saw him today. Very down-and-out he looked."

"Is he at the same boarding-house?"

"No. I went round to see my friend Mrs Salter. He left there at once."

"I'm glad you did that."

"You're not forgetting the farmer chap with the worn brake-cable?"

"I'm not forgetting anyone."

"Then do let's have some action, sir. The thing's gone far enough."

"In your odious lingo—I couldn't agree with you more."

Mrs Stick brought in the tea, and Carolus guessed from the expression on her face that Ethel Pink's visit had not been unobserved. But this was bad diagnosis.

"How are you enjoying Blessington, Mrs Stick?" asked Rupert Priggley mischievously.

"Enjoying it? How can anyone enjoy a place where Stick only has to go out to do a bit of shrimping when he sees the fire brigade and police and all of them out recovering a dead body from the side of the cliff not half a mile from where the other one was found? We shall have one in the wardrobe next, I shouldn't be surprised, if we go on getting mixed up in such things."

She put down the tray and left the room in what Wilde once called 'a marked manner'.

15

THERE were two or three more routine enquiries which Carolus had to make, and the most urgent was an interview with Cupperly the chemist. Carolus believed that on this might depend his whole case. If Cupperly was communicative and accurate and gave certain information which Carolus already suspected, then there would be no more mystery about the death of Lillianne Bomberger. That of Alice Pink was a simpler matter altogether.

But would Cupperly be communicative? Carolus was only too aware of his own amateur status. Whereas the police had only to walk in and show their cards, Carolus had to depend on the goodwill of the chemist, his recognition that Carolus did not come out of idle curiosity and his willingness to give information about his customers' purchases, which in a certain sense was a breach of confidence.

However, Carolus thought he was more likely to get the facts he wanted from Cupperly than from the police, so he set off for the chemist's shop before ten o'clock in the morning, when he thought it would not be too busy.

The shop was in one of the principal streets of the town, but it was not large, and when Carolus entered he was the only customer. That special smell of soap and scent which is common to all English chemists' shops but imperceptible in those abroad, was potent here. One had the impression of walking into an atmosphere sanitary, scrubbed, disinfected and scented. And behind the counter stood the very personification of all this, a fair-haired man with rimless glasses who looked as though he had just come from a vigorous masseur in a hygienic Turkish bath and been shaved and scrubbed and polished. He was about forty years old, and Carolus thought as he saw his shining white coat and brilliant fingernails that there is a kind of personal cleanliness which almost amounts to morbidity.

"What can I get for you, sir?" asked Mr Cupperly without smiling.

"Aspirin," said Carolus. "But I also wanted to ask you a couple of questions."

"Gallup poll?"

"No, no. Professional questions."

"Ah," said Mr Cupperly and looked even more important.

"You see, I'm making a private investigation of the death of Mrs Bomberger."

"Now there, sir, we touch on difficult ground," said Mr Cupperly with some unction. "We approach a delicate question."

"Why?"

"I respect the confidence of my customers. I cannot play fast and loose with information entrusted to me."

"But I'm not asking you to do that."

"When a doctor writes a prescription," went on Mr Cupperly, "he does so in the full confidence that the member of the pharmaceutical profession who is required to make it up will regard it as a sacred trust."

"I'm only asking . . ."

"We do not actually take the Hippocratic oath, but the more conscientious of us feel bound by it."

"The question I want to put . . ."

"In the eleven years I have had this shop I may say that I have never been guilty of the smallest breach of that trust which was laid on me when I became a registered pharmaceutical chemist after satisfying the Pharmaceutical Society and attending an approved systematic course of not less than one thousand six hundred hours in botany, chemistry, pharmacognosy, pharmacy and forensic pharmacy."

"I simply wanted . . ."

"Although I recognize that in cases of sudden decease in which murder is suspected, the pharmacist's knowledge of the deceased person's habits may be valuable to the authorities and should be placed at their disposal I cannot approve of giving details to unauthorized persons."

"But . . ."

"If, of course, you could satisfy me that you have some official status in the matter and come to me with the approval of all concerned, I should feel inclined to waive the formalities and give you the details you require."

"I only want . . ."

"If on the other hand it is in a spirit of mere curiosity, almost one might say in pursuit of a hobby, that you enquire, my lips must remain sealed."

"I have been called in by the family. I really need your information, Mr Cupperly. I think it may enable me to clear this beastly thing up."

"In that case I will do my best. But I think it inadvisable to discuss these matters in the shop. It is early closing day today, and if you would care to call in the afternoon I shall be pleased to assist you."

"Where do you live?" asked Carolus, who was at that moment longing for fresh air.

"We have an apartment in this building. Over the shop, in fact. Four-thirty, I suggest."

"Thank you," said Carolus, and fled from antiseptics and perfumes, Hippocratic oaths and duties to clients, into the fresh air from the North Sea.

But at four-thirty he was back and was led by Mr Cupperly through the side door and up a flight of stairs to a sitting-room as polished as the counter downstairs, its three-ply furniture shining and its very fire-irons having a black glow. Mrs Cupperly, a fierce-looking woman with dark hair and feline movements, sat behind a tea-tray.

"I'm just going to pour out for you, then I'm going down to the beach to pick up the children while you have your natter."

She scarcely waited to hand Carolus bread and butter before she disappeared, clearly by pre-arrangement with her husband.

Mr Cupperly meant to enjoy himself, as Carolus saw at once. He leaned back in his chair, joined the tips of his fingers and said, "Now!"

"I understand that there were three kinds of narcotics . . ."

"Soporifics."

"Soporifics, then, used in that house. Bromaloid, which was taken by Miss Pink in liquid form . . ."

"You can really leave that out. Its chemical contents were not interesting and no one else took it. Miss Pink had the old-fashioned idea that sleeping-pills of any sort were dangerous but a 'dose of medicine' before going to bed would do no one any harm. She never touched any of the others and Bromaloid is the mildest thing we have. A whole bottle wouldn't have hurt her. The effect was psychological."

"I see. Next there were the Komatoza tablets taken by the two sisters."

"Yes. Komatoza is a preparation of pheno-barbitone which can only be sold on a doctor's prescription."

"They had one, of course?"

"Dr Flitcher's. Yes. I supplied them with that regularly, and have done for eighteen months or so."

"You have a full record of your sales to them of it?"

"Yes, I have. And that is what you are going to find interesting, I think. That is why I showed a certain reserve in parting with my information."

"Yes?"

Mr Cupperly referred to certain notes which he had beside him.

"The Stayers started taking Komatoza in January of last year. At first their joint consumption was no more than a dozen tablets a week, but as time went on this increased, until in January of this year they were using twenty tablets a week between them. I'll spare you the details, but these tablets are sold in boxes of twenty-five, and my records, which have to be accurate with pheno-barbitone preparations, enable me to say in weekly terms just what they took."

"Good. That makes it easier for me."

"This consumption did not vary for a long time, then about three months ago it increased. Mrs Bomberger came to me and asked for sleeping-pills of some kind. 'I have had certain business anxieties lately,' she confided in me. 'And sometimes I find I cannot sleep. It is not often that this happens, but I like to be prepared for it when it does.' I asked why she did not try the Komatoza, which her nieces used. She said, 'Well, to tell you the truth I find it quite ineffective. I am possibly a more difficult subject than my nieces.' I then recommended her to consult her doctor, who could give her a prescription for something more effective. Some days later one of her nieces . . ."

"Which?"

"Fortunately I can tell you that, since she had to sign the book. It was Miss Babs Stayer. She brought in Dr Flitcher's prescription for certain sleeping-pills which are only given to patients suffering severe pain or in very obstinate cases of insomnia. They are, like most drugs nowadays, manufactured by one of the great firms and ready for sale under a doctor's certificate. They also are a pheno-barbitone preparation, but with morphine. I gave the niece the usual warning and wrote clearly on the box that not more than one tablet was to be taken at a time. You may know that the Labelling of Poisons Order, which came into force on the first day of January 1926, makes it an offence to sell any preparation containing an ingredient to which the Pharmacy Act applies without stating on the label the proportion of the specified poison to the whole preparation. Needless to say, I have always conformed most scrupulously with this Order."

"Quite, quite."

Undeterred, Mr Cupperly proceeded, "Moreover, the Dangerous Drug Act of 1920–23 lays down that except by a doctor's prescription certain drugs may not be suppplied at all. These are morphine, cocaine, ecgonine, diamorphine, heroin and their respective salts, and medicinal opium. Even when there is a doctor's prescription, a careful register must be kept of these drugs, both of quantities bought by the pharmacist and of those sold by him. You can imagine that in selling these things to Mrs Bomberger I was particularly careful to conform with all orders. I repeated them verbally to Miss Babs Stayer."

I bet you did, thought Carolus, but replied, "Naturally."

"After I had given her the first supply of the tablets prescribed by Dr Flitcher I heard no more from her for some six weeks. But during this time the quantity of Komatoza used by the nieces noticeably increased, until recently it was something over forty tablets a week. I was somewhat perturbed by this and intended to consult Dr Flitcher, but unfortunately it slipped my mind until too late."

"You were telling me about Mrs Bomberger's tablets."

"Oh yes. At the end of six weeks she was supplied again through Miss Babs Stayer, with a second box containing, like the first, twenty tablets. The police inform me that they found this box by her bed with six tablets missing on the day after her death. They brought the box to me, in fact, to identify."

"Thank you, Mr Cupperly. May I say that you are admirably clear and explicit?"

"A pharmacist becomes accustomed to precision, Mr Deene. I see no reason why he should not be as accurate in using words as in making up a prescription."

"I suppose it's a bit out of your province, but do you find anything odd in the fact that poison was still in the dead woman's intestines even after her immersion?"

"It is, as you say, out of my province. The *Fédération Internationale Pharmaceutique* insists that a pharmacist should study a certain number of subjects, but he is not required to be able to conduct post-mortems."

As though he was fascinated by a mesmeric cobra, Carolus heard himself asking what those subjects were and caught the unctuous glee in Mr Cupperly's voice as he answered him.

"Chemistry (analytical, biological, physiological and pathological), pharmacy (chemical and galenical), pharmacognosy, micrography, toxicology, hygiene, legislation, pharmacology, botany, microbiology, mathematics, crystallography, disinfection, sterilization and optics."

"Phew!" said Carolus.

"It is not a profession to be taken up lightly, Mr Deene."

"I should think not!"

"We have a grave responsibility to the public even if, as it may appear, we are mostly concerned with the sale of bath salts and throat pastilles."

"Certainly. What about this weed-killer sold to Miss Stayer?"

"I can't see how that comes into it. The tin had never been opened."

"Just the same, I'm interested."

"It's a very simple matter. Miss Stayer . . ."

"Gracie Stayer, that is?"

Mr Cupperly nodded.

"Miss Stayer was in here one day making another purchase when it seemed suddenly to occur to her. 'Oh, Mr Cupperly,' she said, 'have you got something for weeds?' I asked her what kind of weeds and where they were and she said they were away from all plants, coming up in the gravel. So I gave her an arsenical weed-killer which could be safely used in that garden because there are no dogs or cats. The late Mrs Bomberger detested both, I understand."

"That's all there was to it?"

"Yes. It would never have been heard of again if the police, in enquiring about the sleeping-tablets after Mrs

Bomberger's death, had not asked me whether I had ever supplied any other poison. I felt bound to mention this."

"I see. I'm most grateful for your information . . ."

After another homily, mercifully brief, on the duties and responsibilities of a registered pharmacist, Mr Cupperly let Carolus go.

He decided to call on the doctor whose address he had from the telephone directory. He found Dr Flitcher's house pleasantly set in a large square garden.

A smart young woman dressed as a nurse appeared in answer to his ring.

"May I see Dr Flitcher?" he asked.

"Health Service? Or do you want to see him privately?"

"Oh, privately," said Carolus, who had not needed a doctor since coming out of the army and did not realize the implications of the question.

"Please come this way."

Carolus was left alone in a room with the usual illustrated papers and sank into an arm-chair too deep for him. After a few minutes a tall young man asked him to come in.

"What's the trouble?" asked the young man, waving his stethoscope.

"I'm a private investigator," began Carolus. "I mean I'm interested in unusual deaths . . ."

"Look, I'm a general practitioner, not a psychiatrist."

"Is your name Flitcher?" asked Carolus.

"No. Flitcher's on holiday. I'm his locum."

"If I had known that I needn't have troubled you."

"No trouble. But Flitcher's not a psychiatrist either. With those illusions of yours I should consult someone in Harley Street. They're probably due to something you saw in your nursery."

"Thanks. When will Flitcher be back?"

"Not for another fortnight. But he could only tell you what I have."

"Probably," said Carolus and managed to get himself out of the house.

He had one more chore that day, and he stopped at a telephone-booth to do it. Getting through, after a few moments' delay, to Detective Inspector Whibley, he asked him cheerfully if he had the result yet of the post-mortem on Alice Pink.

"I can't possibly discuss these things, Mr Deene," said the Inspector.

"Why not? You told me . . ."

"Perhaps I might go so far as to say that you were right in your conjecture."

"The same as Bomberger?"

"Now, Mr Deene, I mustn't answer questions from out-siders. You know that perfectly well. But I shouldn't be surprised if it was the same. No, I shouldn't be at all surprised."

"Thank you," said Carolus. "Now I'm going to say something to you. You won't like it, because you'll think I'm not minding my own business, or even that I'm trying to teach you yours. But I'm going to risk offending you and tell you straight out that this thing is not finished and that there is a danger, a very grave danger, of another corpse."

There was a silent pause at the other end, then the receiver was hung up.

16

THE question which Carolus now wanted to resolve was that of the husband, Otto Bomberger. He was inclined to be more interested than the police in this man's presence in Blessington on the night of Lillianne Bomberger's death. He knew enough to be sure that Detective Inspector Whibley would never have given him that piece of information if he thought it anything but a red herring. Yet Carolus was not so sure that there was not a certain involvement of Bomberger. Apart from that, the man might have information of another kind which could be useful.

Carolus wanted a long drive in which to think. Alone in his car, dismissing the miles, he found he could order his ideas and use his imagination far better than at any other time. From Blessington to Brighton was a longish drive, and he would have to go through London, but on the whole he decided in favour of it.

Carolus had always liked Brighton and had a new respect for it as the only coastal resort with the courage to clean up its police force. He intended to stay for only one night and to be in Blessington again on the next evening, but he realized that in order to do this he needed a certain amount of luck in finding Bomberger.

The name the man used now, according to Detective Inspector Whibley, was White, and he was to be found at a pub called the Green Star.

This turned out to be a crowded place with a piano being played by a young man with too much hair, too many airy gestures and too little knowledge of his instrument. The customers were mixed, dressy, criminal-looking or giggly; they had a curiously slick yet raddled look.

Carolus could not make out quite why, but on entering he had a sense not of impending trouble, but of trouble anticipated. The two young ladies behind the bar, the burly landlord who stood in front of it leaning on it to keep some of the weight of his large, sagging body from his feet, the lithe little potman—all these seemed too alert, too watchful.

Carolus stood near the landlord and ordered a large whisky. The landlord said good evening in a hurried, abstracted way, never taking his attention from the crowd. Carolus decided that a direct approach was best.

"D'you know a character who calls himself White?" he asked.

The landlord had started shaking his head before the question was finished.

"Recently been questioned by the police in the Bomberger case?" went on Carolus calmly.

The landlord slowly turned a liverish glance towards Carolus and his headshake was far less decided.

"Known to come here every night. Been in prison once or twice."

From the landlord's swollen throat came a wheezy question.

"Who wants him?" he asked.

"My name's Deene. He won't know me. I only want a chat."

"No rough stuff here," warned the landlord.

"No, no."

"We can't have any trouble here. Only last night we had to have the police in. Started over nothing, and before you knew where you were there were glasses flying."

Carolus nodded understandingly.

"That's the worst of a house like this—you never know. But if I show you which is this White, you won't start anything, will you? Because I won't stand for it. We've had quite enough trouble as it is. Lot of nonsense about who you can serve and who you can't serve. How am I supposed

146

to know? You're standing here having a chat with someone when all of a sudden it's started. That's White. By the piano."

"With the buttonhole?"

"That's it. That short bloke who never stops talking. He's the one you want."

"Thanks."

Carolus eased his way between be-ringed and gesticulating hands, massively tailored shoulders, cigarette-holders and clutched glasses to where the indicated man was standing.

"Mr White? Can I have a word with you?"

How different the cliché sounded here from its use by Mr Gorringer.

The man addressed, a vigorous, overdressed type in his later forties, looked enquiringly at Carolus.

"You the Law?" he asked without embarrassment.

"No."

"Press?"

Carolus shook his head.

"What the hell are you, then?"

"Connected with the Bomberger case."

"Solicitor?"

"No. But I know the family."

"Come outside of this. Can't talk here, with this din going on."

They found their way to the door, and just as they stepped on the pavement there was the crash of broken glass behind them which everyone seemed to have been anticipating.

"There they go," said Bomberger. "Every night. Let's pop into the Yellow Lion. We can get a quiet drink in there. What is it you want to know?"

"Chiefly, and without wasting time, whether you telephoned your wife from Blessington at about ten o'clock on the night of her death?"

"Wait a minute. Wait a minute. Who says she was my wife?"

"The marriage is registered. I can't find any evidence of divorce. I know your name's Bomberger, of course."

"Know a bloody lot, don't you?" said Bomberger in a perfectly friendly way. "If I knew as much as you I shouldn't need to ask any questions. I don't mind. I've told the police, so I may as well tell you. Yes, I'm Bomberger. Only down here there's no one knows me as anything but White. You didn't say anything to that landlord, did you? I saw you speaking to the windy old so-and-so."

"No. Nothing."

"Good. Well, I was born Bomberger, but I can't say I fancy the name now. I married Lil more than twenty years ago, before she was anything or looked like being. I'll tell you a funny thing. I married her because I was sorry for her and she married me because she thought I was going to get somewhere, be someone. And it's gone just the other way about. *She* went up and I went down, and if you'd seen the two of us on the day we got married you'd never have believed it would turn out like that. Yes, I'll have a gin and soda."

"You did some time, didn't you?"

"Three lots altogether. I only came out from the last about six months ago. But that's not why we parted. I couldn't stick it, old chap. Not Lil, I couldn't. I've never found anyone who could. Soon as she began to make money she got worse. In the end I told her, I said, 'I wouldn't stay with you, Lil, if you were making a million a year out of your books. You're the end.' And I went. Left her going right up, but I was glad to get out. Then I got mixed up in this diamond-smuggling lark. Some dirty grass done me and I got two years. When I came out I found she was the great Lillianne Bomberger. She'd kept the name because it had been too late to change it.

"I never went near her. Funny thing, but although I had a bad time for a while I didn't want anything from her. And this last time when I came out it was her who got in touch with me."

"Was it indeed?" Carolus was not sceptical, but interested.

"Yes. Sent for me down to Blessington and saw me there. Told me to come up to the house at a certain time as though I was selling something and not give my real name and she would see me. She did. My gawd, old chap, you should have watched her. It was a picture."

"Why?"

"You never knew her, did you? Pleased with herself and sneering at the same time. 'It's most distasteful to me to receive you, Otto. I want simply to make a business proposition to you.' 'I'm always open to that,' I said. What d'you think it was she wanted me to do? Change my name. Anything for Bomberger. She was afraid of me going inside again, and of course she couldn't change hers. She wanted it done properly so that if I was nicked they couldn't say 'Bomberger alias White' or anything. She gave me a hundred nicker on account and promised me five hundred when it was through, she paying lawyer's charges. I was willing enough on those terms and told her so. So she said I was to come back when it was all settled and she'd give me the rest. That's why I was in Blessington that night. I'd only arrived in the afternoon, as I proved to the police."

"So you telephoned?"

"Yes. At ten o'clock."

"Why did you give the name Green?"

"It was an old joke of ours, if you could imagine such a thing as a joke with Lil. She used to call me 'Mr Green' when we were married. Green light. Go ahead. See?"

"Yes, I see."

"I was in a hurry that night. I wanted to get back to Brighton. I'd written her ahead to say I was coming and to have the lolly ready in ones. But when I got through to her she couldn't see anything but her own convenience, of course. 'I can't possibly see you tonight,' she said. 'I've already come up to bed and taken my sleeping-pills. I'll

149

see you tomorrow.' She sounded perfectly calm and smug; her usual self, in fact. I told her I wanted to get back here. I do a bit on the race-course, you see, and didn't like missing two days. But no. 'You may come at noon tomorrow, ostensibly on the same business as last time. I shall require all the evidence, of course.' "

"Did you go up next day?"

"No. By a lucky chance I heard what had happened. It was beginning to be talked about in the town. I'm glad I didn't now, otherwise I might have been mixed up in it. As it was I missed the five hundred quid and came straight back to Brighton."

"You never went near the house at all?"

"No. Not that time."

"Thank you for all you have told me. You've given me a most valuable piece of information."

Bomberger nodded.

"I think she might have left me something," he said. "We didn't get on, but after all I married her when no one else would. However, it's all in a life."

"What makes you think she hasn't?"

"Scarcely likely."

"I don't want to raise your hopes for nothing, but I seem to remember hearing that a sum was left to you."

Bomberger became a new man, lively and insistent.

"Do you really, old man? Cast your mind back now. Are you sure about that? How much do you seem to remember it was? Take it steady now and try to think. This means a lot to me. Do you think it might have been a thousand quid?"

"I don't think any sum was mentioned."

"I mean, a thousand quid would come in very handy just now. Very handy indeed. You don't think it was as much as two thousand, do you? No, she'd never have left me two thousand, the mean cow."

"It may have been no more than a token payment, for all I can say."

"Token payment, old man? What's a token payment? Token of what?"

"Of her goodwill towards you."

"I don't like the sound of that. How much is a token payment?"

"It might be anything. It might be just a nominal sum with which to buy mourning . . ."

"Mourning? She didn't think I'd go into mourning for her if she hadn't left me more than that, did she?"

"I really don't know," said Carolus, who was inwardly smiling for the first time in several long, hard-working days. "I can't remember at all what the sum was. It may have been no more than a couple of hundred pounds."

The thermometer, having dropped to zero, began to rise again.

"A couple of hundred? Well, that would be better than a kick in the pants. But surely if she was leaving me a couple of hundred she'd have made it a round sum like five, wouldn't she? Bit more dignity to it then. She was always a woman for dignity. I can't see how you're so sure it wasn't a thousand. That's the sort of sum Lil would have chosen, just to show she'd got it."

"I'm not sure," said Carolus. "I don't remember at all."

"Then it probably is a thousand, if I know Lil. She was a four-figure woman, if you know what I mean. She wouldn't have left me anything at all if it wasn't a thousand or more. Or more. You can't be certain it wasn't two, can you?"

"No, I can't," admitted Carolus. "I can't be certain there was a bequest at all."

"What do you mean, old chap? You've just been telling me there's a bequest. Don't go back on your word now."

"I said I seemed to remember there was."

"Then there may be nothing at all? Not a bloody fiver? Nice thing to leave her husband without a penny."

"A few minutes ago you seemed quite resigned to it. You said it was all in a life."

"Yes, but that was before you started leading me on, old

151

man. It was you who put the idea into my head. I mean, I wouldn't mind so long as there's just something. You know, something worth waiting for. Like the five hundred nicker she promised me for changing my name."

"There's one way you could find out. The executor is still down at Blessington. George Stump, her publisher. He would be able to tell you exactly and you could explain to him about the five hundred pounds."

"I could, couldn't I? Are you going back tomorrow? How about taking me along?"

"You can come," said Carolus.

"I mean, it's worth taking a chance, isn't it?"

"You would then be there when the case closes."

"Yes. I'm not so much interested in that. But a nice little sum would come just at the right time."

"When doesn't it?" agreed Carolus. "All right, tomorrow at nine-thirty. Call for me at the Old Ship."

The drive back to Blessington was less tiresome than Carolus supposed. Bomberger's spirits rose and fell like mercury and took them through London and out to Suffolk without flagging. Carolus asked a few desultory questions about the past, but he knew quite enough of the late Lillianne Bomberger, and did not want more details of her sordidly successful career.

Dropping Bomberger at Peep O'Day, he made for Wee Hoosie, where he found a letter waiting for him addressed in the unmistakable handwriting of Mr Gorringer.

                                        Pension Le Balmoral,
                                                    Ostende.

My dear Deene,

        I have just received a most disturbing letter from Mr George Stump, a director of the firm of Stump and Agincourt. He tells me that not only are you immersed in the investigation of the most unfortunate death of Lillianne Bomberger the novelist, but that you actually appear to consider him almost as one of your so-called suspects.

I do not need to repeat here my strong disapproval of your meddling in matters which concern only the police or my constant anxiety lest in doing so you once again allow the name of the Queen's School, Newminster to be associated with events so foreign to the education of the young. I write to you this time with another, perhaps more personal, apprehension.

You may not be aware that I have at last succumbed to the myriad solicitations and hopes expressed by people in many walks of life, governors, masters and old boys of the school, eminent scholars and distinguished persons who have known me and a host of others, and committed to paper my memoirs.

The book, which I have entitled *The Wayward Mortarboard or Thirty Years on the Slopes of Parnassus*, is actually in print; indeed I have dedicated much of my vacation to correcting the proofs. This book is to be published by the very firm one of the partners in which you seem to have so rashly and inconsiderately involved in your capricious investigations. I am horrified and dismayed to realize this, and in the circumstances have decided to cut short my holiday in Ostende and betake myself immediately to Blessington-on-Sea to learn the truth of the matter and if possible avert any worse calamity. I shall arrive on Monday next at 3.15 p.m. and shall be obliged if you will meet me at the railway station.

Yours sincerely but apprehensively,
Hugh Gorringer.

17

CAROLUS spent an almost sleepless night and rose before breakfast to drive to his cousin's hotel.

"Look, Fay, I've decided to throw this case up."

"My dear, you can't."

"I've quite made up my mind. I'm going to leave Blessington tomorrow."

"And the case unsolved?"

"I'm not going to propound any solution. I've had a rotten night, Fay, and I've found this an ugly case from the start. I want to get away to a holiday somewhere else."

"What about the two unfortunate nieces?"

"I'll go up this morning and tell them what I've decided. You might go first and prepare them. Do you think you could get the Cribbs to the house?"

"I daresay."

"Try, will you? I'm going to bring George Stump and the husband."

"Whose, Carolus? You're more vague than I am this morning."

"Lillianne Bomberger's. He was in Blessington on the night of her death."

"I see. You want a meeting of suspects."

"Call it what you like. I want to tell these people I'm throwing up the case and why."

He went back to Wee Hoosie for breakfast and sharply told Mrs Stick some news which for her would be excellent.

"I'm giving up this case, Mrs Stick."

"I'm glad to hear it. I'm not saying it's been as bad as some of them when people were ringing the bell all day and

I never knew who they might be. But it's been bad enough, and I'm thankful to hear you're not going on with it." Mrs Stick paused for a moment, then astonishingly added, "Can't you find out who did it?"

"Never mind that. We shall leave here as soon as possible."

"There. And I was just getting used to moving the furniture about every time I wanted to cross the room."

Carolus went after breakfast to pick up George Stump at the Palatial.

"Yes, I don't mind coming out," he said, "but I'm sorry you're not going to finish the job. It doesn't look as though the police are getting much farther, so perhaps we never shall know whether Lillianne and Alice Pink were murdered and if so, by whom."

Bomberger was called for at Peep O'Day, and Carolus and Stump had to wait while he roused himself and dressed.

"I should like you to come out to the house," said Carolus. "I have something to explain which I think will interest you."

Bomberger did not hesitate to get into the car, but, to avoid a wearisome catechism of George Stump at this point, Carolus did not introduce the two men.

At Trumbles Carolus found that Fay had succeeded, for Gracie and Babs Stayer were with Ron and Gloria Cribb in the large room which Lillianne Bomberger had not scrupled to call the lounge. Carolus was interested to see that unless all five of them were brilliant actors Bomberger and his relatives by marriage were complete strangers.

There were a good many anxious looks towards Carolus, and he said at last: "I'm sorry if I am disappointing anyone or breaking any sort of verbal or implied contract, but I've decided to resign from this case."

"Defeated?" suggested Gloria Cribb.

"I don't quite know how to answer that. I know who killed Lillianne Bomberger and where and why. I know

155

why she was buried in the sand and by whom. I also know who killed Alice Pink and how and why."

"Then why are you running away?" persisted Gloria.

"Because I could not prove any of it. Both murders were ingenious and lucky, and it may be that no charge will be brought until the police obtain a certain piece of evidence which I do not wish to obtain. Please don't ask me what it is, for if I answered that I should be revealing more than I ought. I will say only that it *can* be obtained, that it almost certainly will be, but that it is not for me to obtain it."

"But if you can't prove it, how can you say you know?"

"Perhaps I don't, as Euclid knew things. But I'm as sure as Einstein. I mean, I'm satisfied, anyway. But every scrap of evidence I have is circumstantial, and I cannot make it anything else. If the Detective Inspector in charge of the case wishes me to do so I shall tell him my conclusions. On the other hand he may know very well and be about to act on what he knows. I cannot. It would entail doing something which I am constitutionally incapable of doing."

"Do you think the police *are* so advanced?" asked George Stump incredulously.

"I don't know. There is a basic difference between their approach to the problem and mine. I am trying to find out who has committed a murder. They are looking for the chance of a successful prosecution. I do not mean that they would go out to get an innocent man convicted. It would be too difficult, for one thing. It's hard enough when he's guilty. I mean, they want to know who is the murderer because it's easier to prove a case against him than against anyone else. The whole business of the British police force is not what it was founded for, the maintenance of law and order, but getting convictions. A murder case is no exception."

"And you don't think they'll obtain one here unless they get, or have already got, the mysterious piece of evidence you mention?" asked George Stump.

"That's what I think."

"So you're leaving?"

"Tomorrow, yes."

"Haven't you suggested that there might be yet another murder?" asked Gloria.

"I have, yes."

"And you think you are justified in leaving?"

"Certainly. I could do nothing to prevent it."

"Except say what you know. That would prevent it, wouldn't it?"

"I doubt it. I hope what will prevent it is that the murderer will realize the futility of going on. A murderer who sets out to eliminate everyone with evidence against him may end by having to take a Sten gun to an entire population. It's a snowball process as the information is passed on."

"Do you suggest any precautions that might be taken?"

"Only the elementary one on which I have been insisting ever since I came here—tell the truth. If everyone had told the truth from the first, Alice Pink would be alive. If everyone tells it now, at once, to the police, there will be no more murders."

"Otherwise, you maintain, there may be?" asked George Stump.

"Otherwise there may. I'm sorry I can do no more."

Back at Wee Hoosie he found Priggley waiting.

"You're not really throwing in the sponge are you?"

"Yes. Really."

"But you can't possibly. I've got more than a tenner out on your solving before the police. Apart from that you'll never, in the language of your favourite authors, be able to lift your head again."

"I want nothing more to do with it and I've told them so. The headmaster arrives this afternoon, by the way."

"You don't say! Why has he abandoned Ostende, with days spent in Bruges?"

"He's worried about my investigations."

"Is *that* why you've thrown up the case?"

"You know the answer to that."

"Of course I do. But he'll be tickled pink to hear you've chucked it."

"But not that he has come home for nothing."

Carolus found that afternoon that Mr Gorringer's feelings about the situation were not quite as he had anticipated.

"Ah, Deene," he greeted Carolus severely as he alighted from a third-class compartment. "Able to meet me, I rejoice to see. And splendid weather. Splendid. Only the one suit-case. I hope not to have to make a long stay. Ah, thank you. I am at your disposal. Whither?"

"I've booked a room for you at the Seaview Hotel. I thought your wife would be with you."

"No. Mrs Gorringer has remained in Ostende. Now I am most anxious to have a few words with you, Deene. Most anxious. You, I gather, have taken a furnished house here?"

"That is an exaggeration. But we will go to it, and you can see for yourself. It is called Wee Hoosie."

"Ah, Scottish, I perceive," said the headmaster brightly, then seemed to recollect himself. "But we have graver things to discuss than house names."

"Mrs Stick will give us a cup of tea and you can get whatever it is off your chest," said Carolus.

"I cannot altogether approve of the levity with which you speak, Deene. It is not to 'get something off my chest' that I have abandoned a well-earned vacation in Ostende. It is to prevent, if possible, a major calamity, for you, for me, for the school and for the distinguished firm of Stump and Agincourt. I trust I am not too late."

In the 'front room' Mr Gorringer looked large and out of place.

"Far be it from me," he said after an awed glance at the wedding groups—"far be it from me to feel surprise at any *pied-à-terre* you may wish to choose, but I cannot help asking

158

what induced you to rent such—may I say?—unsuitable apartments? Superabundance of furniture seems the most striking feature of your temporary home, my dear Deene."

"It's through her having come into all her sister's things just after their mother died."

"Ah, heirlooms," said Mr Gorringer. "Now, Deene, what is this distressing business? I understand there has been a second death. The secretary."

"Quite true."

"You seem extraordinarily composed about it. I should have thought that a second demise in a case which you are investigating was not only a tragedy in itself but a reflection on your abilities."

"I suppose it is, but the silly women would not tell me the truth."

"The secretary's name, I read in my newspaper, was Alice Pink. She had relatives, I hope?"

"A sister. Rather your type, headmaster."

"I beg your pardon, Deene. May I ask what you mean by 'my type'?"

"Oh, I meant professionally. She's the matron of a preparatory school. I should think a splendid one."

"Indeed? By a strange coincidence I heard only a few days ago that our trusted Mrs Critchley is not returning to us next term."

"Grab this one then. You and she were made for one another. In a purely professional sense, of course."

Mr Gorringer coughed.

"To return to our muttons," he said. "What I am most anxious to know, indeed I do not exaggerate when I say that I am on tenterhooks to know, is whether Mr George Stump is in any way involved in this regrettable affair?"

"I don't know. I resigned from it this morning. I want nothing more to do with it."

The headmaster blinked.

"Can you be serious, Deene? Resigned, before the truth

has been revealed? I almost said, deserted in the face of the enemy."

"You've always told me that you wanted me to leave these things to the police. In the letter I received from you yesterday you reiterated this. I have decided to do as you suggest."

"But, Deene, there is a sharp distinction between keeping yourself clear of a thing of this kind and leaving it in mid-stream. I find your conduct, if I may go so far, savours of pusillanimity. It leaves Mr Stump in a position which at any moment may lead to his interrogation and conceivably even some mistaken suspicion on the part of the police."

"Oh, I should think he's a suspect. The police have questioned him, anyway."

"You cannot mean it! This is indeed alarming. I trust you told them that he is engaged at present in the most important matters of publishing? What possible reason can they have had for interrogating Mr Stump?"

"He went up to the house that evening."

"An unfortunate coincidence, nothing more. Anyone might have gone up to the house that evening. I might have myself."

"You were in Ostende. Or was it one of your days in Bruges? A long way from here, at all events."

"I sometimes find you sadly lacking in a sense of humour, Deene. I was using myself merely as an illustration of the absurdity of questioning Mr Stump for no better reason than that he visited the house on the night of Mrs Bom-berger's death. Did he see the lady?"

"No. She had given orders that he must not be admitted."

"You see? Typical police blundering. The sort of thing of which you, my dear Deene, would never be guilty, in spite of your occasional lapses of taste, if I may make so bold as so to describe them."

"Apart from the fact that you have repeatedly told me that the police know their own business best, I myself grilled George Stump most thoroughly."

"Then I despair of you!" cried Mr Gorringer. "I have rarely heard anything more far-fetched."

"At all events, I'm out of it now. They can arrest whom they like, so far as I'm concerned."

"You use words very lightly, Deene. You are not suggesting, I trust, that the police might even—but of course it is preposterous—might even go so far in monstrous folly as to *apprehend* Mr Stump?"

"If they think he is guilty, they will. He was in the middle of a most violent quarrel with Lillianne Bomberger."

"Pooh! Royalties and dust-jackets!"

"But to a woman of Lillianne Bomberger's kind every quarrel was one to the death."

"What extravagant phrases you employ, Deene. But let us dispute no more. The important thing is that you should quickly, nay instantly, resume your investigations in order to solve this most infelicitous affair and reveal the truth in the shortest possible time, thus saving Mr Stump from any possibility of embarrassment."

"Can't do that, I'm afraid, headmaster. I've finished with it. Glad to be, in fact. It's a beastly business."

"Pardon me, Deene. But I do not think that you can have realized the full implications. I, your headmaster, to whom you owe at least a measure of loyalty and consideration, have entrusted the child of my brain, the fruit of a life-time's experience, the composium of my varied interests and speculations, to the firm of which Mr Stump is the senior partner. Early next spring Stump and Agincourt are due to publish *The Wayward Mortar-board*."

"*Or Thirty Years on the Slopes of Parnassus*. I know. But I can't do anything about it. I don't see it would make much difference, anyhow. Agincourt would carry on even if Stump were nicked."

"Deene! I forbid you to employ this flippancy in a matter of such vital moment. But let us be calm. Do you know that Mrs Bomberger was murdered?"

"Yes. But I can't prove it."

"Do you know who was guilty of that crime?"

"Yes. But again I have only circumstantial evidence."

"And Miss Pink?"

"The same applies."

"Was it the same person?"

"I think so, yes."

"Then prove it, man! Prove it. It should be a challenge to you!"

"I'm sorry, headmaster; I'm leaving Blessington tomorrow. For good."

But that Carolus was unable to do. For in the morning, before Mrs Stick had finished packing, the little town rang with the news that there had been another death at Trumbles. Babs Stayer was found in bed in the morning, having died some hours previously.

The cause of death was confidently thought to be an overdose of sleeping-pills containing morphine, a conclusion which was afterwards confirmed by autopsy. So for Carolus his escape became impossible.

18

CAROLUS remained all that day in the stuffy front room of the house he had so rashly rented, at first refusing to see anyone. But when Priggley arrived about noon, Mrs Stick obtained his unwilling permission to admit him.

"Achilles sulking in his tent," said Priggley. "And small wonder. I don't know which looks sillier, you or the police. How many more people do you expect to be poisoned? We've only had three green bottles hanging on the wall as yet."

"The headmaster is here," said Carolus. "He arrived yesterday."

"It only needed that. Look, sir, are you going to give your theory of the case now? I frankly don't see how you can do anything else."

"I suppose so. If the police want me to."

They were interrupted by knocking at the front door, and Rupert went to open it. Almost before he had done so Mrs Plum had passed him and was inside.

"Wait a minute. Let me get my breath," she said. "I didn't want any of them to see me coming here, though one or another's bound to have been on the watch." She walked into the room as she spoke and nodded to Carolus. "What did I tell you? I saw it coming from the first. The lady from next door told me just now, when I was putting my washing out. 'I suppose you've heard what's happened now where you were working?' she said, and I told her anything could happen up there. 'Another one gone,' she said, and told me it was Babs. I wasn't surprised, mind you, after what I've seen, but it gave me a nasty turn, all the same—I could hear my heart going bang, bang, bang

163

and thought my legs would crumble under me. So I nipped round to hear what you had to say about it."

"Nothing," said Carolus wearily.

It seemed that Mrs Plum had not heard.

"It's a nice thing, isn't it?" she reflected. "You start with one Going and you never know where it will end. I saw her yesterday morning, too. In the High Street, she was, just coming out of Cupperly's. I little thought it would be the last time I'd set eyes on her, poor thing. It's enough to make anyone feel queer, isn't it? Poisoning anyone like that. I wonder whatever people do it for. Oh well, I must get back. I thought I'd just pop round."

After peering furtively from the door, Mrs Plum made a dash for it.

But not ten minutes later Carolus had another visitor.

"Eyt was almost empossible to faind your hading-place, Mr Deene, though Ey hed the eddress. Ey have a little enformation for you."

"Oh. Do sit down. I'd really given up the case."

"Ey know. Et must be fratefully complicated. End so many daying. Ey'm sure you must be quate worn out. Ey thought jest in case mey little piece of enformation mate be helpful Ey would neep een end tell you."

"Thanks."

"Oh, not et ell. Et's just that the lady who has now dayed, Miss Bebs Stayer, Ey mean, keem into the hotel yesterday. For a dreenk, Ey fency. She went to the Bavarian Weinstube; thet es one of our bars."

Carolus nodded.

"Et must have been about twelve meed-dey. Soon she was joined bey anether lady and gentleman whom Ey know by sate. A farmer neemed Cribb and hes wafe. Very nace people, also connected with Mrs Bomberger, Ey believe."

"Yes. He is."

"Thet es ell, reelly. Ey jest thought you should know."

"Thank you."

"Thenk *you*. Ey can faynd mey way out, thenk you. Goodbey."

The door closed quietly behind her, and her pinnacle heels could be heard on the pavement.

"Ey'd lake to strengle her," said Priggley. "Though I suppose she was trying to be useful. I should think that the news would just about have come to the ears of the head-master and we shall have *him* trundling round. Ah well, never a dull moment."

It was not, however, until after lunch that Mr Gorringer arrived, and when he did so it was with Miss Ethel Pink. Between them they filled the small room.

"Miss Pink chanced to be staying at the same hotel," said Mr Gorringer, "and I was lucky enough to gather her identity from a reference by the hall porter. A natural affinity of anxieties in this most deplorable business, Deene, brought us into conversation."

"Good. I thought you would get on," said Carolus cheerfully.

"But this is no time to be talking of anything but the new and appalling development. What have you to say of that?"

"Nothing. I told you yesterday I had left the case."

"Come, Deene, you can scarcely expect to throw off your responsibilities now that things have taken this ugly turn. You owe it to Miss Pink to give her the fullest details in the matter of her sister's death. You owe it to everyone to explain the truth about Mrs Bomberger. And you have a double, a triple obligation in the matter of this latest tragedy."

"If the police want the results of my work on the case they can have them. But I'm not anxious to give them to anyone else."

"Come, Deene, this is not like you. You have always presented to an audience of those concerned a spirited account of your investigations. You have never failed to keep those who heard you in suspense until in the fullness of time you revealed the murderer's identity. Why not again?"

"It's not that kind of case. It's a sickener this time."

"All the same, I feel it is the appropriate gesture. By it you rid yourself of all responsibilities and can leave Blessington-on-Sea without regret. I suggest my hotel as the *venue* and six o'clock this evening as the time. I will make myself responsible for the presence of all concerned."

"If the police want it," said Carolus. "Only if the police will agree to be there."

"I will make it my business to see them at once. I will also see whether I can persuade Mr George Stump to lend his presence. Who knows but that on hearing your exposition he might express some interest in a written account of the whole crime? That indeed would be a feather in your cap, Deene." He seemed to remember suddenly that he had Ethel Pink with him. "But your first obligation is to relieve, so far as you are able, the doubts and difficulties of the bereaved."

"You really want to know what happened to your sister?" Carolus asked.

Ethel Pink stiffened.

"Of course! What else?"

"It won't make pleasant hearing."

"It won't scare me, if that's what you think. Nine years at St Mervyn's would cure anyone of being frightened too easily by words."

"I wasn't thinking of your being scared."

"Or shocked either. If you had had to deal with assistant masters like ours you'd be unshockable. So you can tell me whatever you think about poor Alice."

"It seems to me that Miss Pink speaks for all," put in Mr Gorringer. "In view of this latest outrage I do not think that even members of the stricken family will wish you to practise reserve. Let us have the truth, the whole truth . . . I need not complete the quotation."

"You shall hear the results of my enquiries."

"Miss Pink should be a lesson to us all in the fortitude with which she bears her burden. It need be no secret from you, Deene, that last night I offered to Miss Pink the vacancy on our staff occasioned by the departure from our ranks of Mrs Critchley and she has accepted. The headmaster of St Mervyn's, whom she has so loyally served, implied a certain criticism of her in a letter she recently received, actually suggesting that she is the cause of his losing so many assistant masters. As I pointed out, what are assistant masters when it is a question of a proficient matron? Miss Pink resented this criticism and has agreed to join us at the beginning of the new term."

"Splendid," said Carolus sincerely, thinking how appropriate the arrangement was.

"Now we must be gone. There are arrangements to be made for your little—*séance*, shall we say?"

When the echoes of their footsteps had died, Priggley said, "Thank God I'm not a boarder. You really are going through with it? Audience and all?"

"Why not? If the police agree."

"I suppose it's all right. Seems a bit gruesome, with last night's corpse scarcely cold, as Mrs Plum would say."

"Murder is gruesome. Now I want you to round up the squint-eyed character Poxton. Also Bomberger. I don't know where you'll find Poxton, but Bomberger's at Peep O'Day."

"Right."

"Make sure they're there this evening. And Primmley. But not Graveston. I want no one from Trumbles. Mrs Plum. George Stump. Cupperly. My cousin Fay."

"I'll do my best. It's not a big lot this time, is it? Not like some of your parties."

"No. It's not."

"You sound pretty sour about it all."

"I am."

When he was left alone, idly shuffling his notes of the case without re-reading them, Carolus felt none of the gusto with which he usually approached his exposition of a crime. This had been from the first an unsatisfactory affair, into which he had been drawn against his instincts by the coincidence that his cousin had discovered the body.

It was impossible to feel anything but sympathy for those who had lived with Lillianne Bomberger, and though by no process of muddled thinking could this sympathy be turned to a palliative for any murderous intentions they might have formed, yet it was impossible to feel quite the same anger over the murder of Lillianne Bomberger as over that of someone kind and selfless.

Then had gone up the blank wall of lies against which he could make so little progress culminating in the death of Alice Pink on the night before she was to have told him everything.

He had been tempted then to leave the case. It had none of the particular subtleties he most enjoyed unravelling. He saw it for what it was, a clever and unscrupulous piece of work for which, it seemed to him, the one responsible might easily escape the consequences. But he had gone on until too late, and the third death had followed so closely on his resignation that he could not now retire from the scene without giving his own conclusions.

However, as he admitted, he had asked for it. He had deliberately come to this unpleasant little town, and he could not deny that it was because he loved criminal investigation for its own sake. Now he must take the consequences.

When Mrs Stick brought in his tea he knew that she, too, had reached that point of exasperation at which she might easily and once and for all give notice.

"We really can get away tomorrow, Mrs Stick. Unless you and Stick like to stay down here for a while and have a real holiday while I go abroad?"

"Stay down here, sir? There isn't neither of us would think of it for a moment. Stick says he scarcely dare push his shrimping-net in the sea for fear of bringing up another corpse, and I don't want to stay in the place a minute longer than I can help, I'm sure. It's got so as no one knows who's going to be next."

"I quite understand. You would like to return to Newminster?"

"As fast as ever the train can carry us. The party next door where we've put the furniture was only saying this morning when we heard the news, 'Well, your gentleman,' she said, 'doesn't seem to have done much good, does he? Another one Passed On, and it wouldn't surprise me if there was more on the way.' It's not very nice for me to hear such things about where I work."

"No. I'm sure it isn't."

"Still, it's to be hoped you've had enough not to want to get mixed up in anything more for a bit, and that's a blessing, anyway. We've got everything packed and ready to go tomorrow."

"Good."

Carolus decided to lie down for an hour's rest before facing the ordeal that lay ahead of him, but at a quarter to six he was ready and drove round to Seaview.

He found Mr Gorringer waiting in the small entrance hall of the hotel.

"I have not had the pleasure of meeting your cousin, Deene. I understand that she is well known in the theatrical profession."

"Fay? Yes, she's quite a star in her way. She's staying here and should be around somewhere. Is there anywhere in this hotel where people sit?"

"Beyond the dining-room there does not appear to be much accommodation. I have arranged for us to use a room on the first floor called the Residents' Lounge, which will be reserved for us. I have seen Detective Inspector Whibley, who will be here in a moment, though he appears to treat this occasion with levity."

"Can't we get a drink?"

"Not until six o'clock, I fear. I myself feel the need of some refreshment in these distressing circumstances."

"Here's Fay. Mr Gorringer, Fay. He likes to be in at the kill."

Mr Gorringer bowed and attempted a smile.

"Your cousin," he said to Fay, "has a most unfortunate way of speaking of these things. It is true that on more than one occasion I have been present when he has made his ... exposition. But not always with pleasure. I cannot take the same view as he does in these affairs."

"Carolus is incorrigible. I asked him down because I was sorry for the unfortunate women out at Trumbles, and now two of them are dead."

"Sad, I know. But I feel it only fair to Deene to hear his explanation before condemning him. Let us now withdraw a little while those concerned are arriving. It will save a great deal of embarrassment, I think."

At six o'clock a young lady in black lace opened a small bar at the end of the passage and Carolus was able to fortify himself with a large whisky and soda.

"I have no doubt that there will be surprises, eh, Deene?"

"Oh, I don't know. It's fairly obvious, really. Anyone who knows all the facts should be able to say at this moment exactly how it happened and who is responsible."

They finished their drinks, and at ten past six went up to the Residents' Lounge to find their audience almost complete. Detective Inspector Whibley smiled broadly to Carolus, as though to excuse his attendance at something so frivolous. Mrs Plum, away in a corner, obviously had her heart in her mouth, if not shivers running up and down her spine. Cupperly had brought his fierce-looking wife. The Matron-to-be of the Queen's School, Newminster looked severe and George Stump bland and expansive. Bomberger and Poxton had apparently made friends. No one was present from Trumbles itself, or rom what Mr Gorringer called the afflicted family, but Primmley was there and so was Rupert Priggley.

"Now, Deene," said Mr Gorringer, and there could be no more delay. Carolus took the plunge.

19

"When I began to look into the death and burial of Lillianne Bomberger, the first thing I noticed was the conspiracy of lies which surrounded it. I will tell you what lies I mean in a moment, but in the meantime I want to say why they seemed significant. This was a matter of life and death and of the macabre discovery of a woman's corpse. If anyone lies in a case like this it can only be with very good reason. Nobody tells a series of prearranged lies for appearances' sake.

"That does not mean that anyone who lies is a murderer —of course not. He may lie to cover up someone or something or some act which has no direct connection with the murder. But if one can distinguish his lies and discover why he is telling them, one is going to come pretty near to a solution.

"I spoke of a conspiracy of lies, and I soon realized it existed, though I could not tell at first whom it embraced. Certainly some women were concerned in the burial of Mrs Bomberger. No man alone could have dressed her correctly in the very elaborate clothes she wore when she was discovered, and if she dressed herself Miss Pink in the next room must have heard her. Besides, when I reached Trumbles all three of the women there were obviously scared and obviously concealing information.

"Take Gracie's shoes, for instance. It occurred to me that if she had gone down to the beach when Mrs Bomberger was buried she would be unlikely to stop to put on plimsolls or anything. So I asked her what shoes she had worn and quickly perceived that she had not her answers ready. She contradicted herself several times, said the shoes were nearly new, that she had given them to Mrs Plum . . ."

"That was a lie if ever there was one," Mrs Plum could not help interrupting, "because she never gave me nothing of the sort, and if she had of done it would of given me the shivers to have worn them, thinking where they might have been!"

"Then," went on Carolus, "she said she had thrown them away, and so on. Babs tried to repair the damage next day, but only succeeded in showing that she was in the conspiracy too.

"Then, whatever lies they had prepared for their movements, they had forgotten to arrange what they should say about the morning. Gracie Stayer, having used an unfortunate phrase about not being disturbed 'until', had to say that Babs had come to wake her at eleven, whereas Babs said that having read a few pages of Mr Gorringer's forthcoming book instead of taking sleeping-pills, she slept right on till Mrs Plum called her to say the police had arrived . . ."

"I can afford to let that pass," rumbled the headmaster. "Critical opinion from those to whom I showed the manuscript has been encouraging enough to make the woman's statement an absurdity. Besides, you are showing her to be untruthful. Proceed, Deene."

"Miss Pink's interrogation came after the others, and there had been time to give her the most plausible story of the three. But these were only some of the lies. No one admitted to hearing anything unusual during the night, or leaving his or her room. Yet between 10 p.m. and the next morning the following things must have happened:

"Lillianne Bomberger was dressed in an elaborate gown.
"She was taken out of the house and down to the beach (for we know that, having taken so many sleeping-pills, she could not possibly have gone out herself).
"Though Miss Pink denied having entered Mrs Bom-

berger's room that night, we know from her letter to her sister that she had actually given her sleeping-pills.

"The key of the drinks cupboard had been brought from Mrs Bomberger's room and some whisky and other drinks consumed.

"The glasses used for this, besides ash-trays, had been washed up.

"The bath-chair kept in the outer scullery had been cleaned.

"A light had been switched on in the potting-shed and shortly afterwards switched off again.

"Now I don't think you will call it exaggeration when I say there was a conspiracy of lies. One or two people might conceivably have slept through this and had no concern with its events—a whole household could not have. But everyone in this household, including the Cribbs, who stayed the night, and Graveston, who was employed there, told the same lies. Therefore—and this was an interesting conclusion—*everyone was in the conspiracy.*"

"Are you going to tell us," broke in George Stump, "that Lillianne Bomberger was killed by a conspiracy of six people?"

"I haven't said anything about her being killed. I said only that there was a conspiracy, and I say now that it was to bury her in the way she was buried."

"Good God! But why?"

"Please let me answer that question when I come to it. I have admitted that much I shall tell you is supported only by circumstantial evidence. I must reconstruct events as I see them.

"At about two o'clock that morning it was discovered—by whom we do not yet know—that Lillianne Bomberger was dead. This caused an extraordinary flutter among those present in the house, and they met in what is called the large sitting-room to discuss the matter. Someone

173

suggested that they needed a drink and someone fetched the key of the drinks cupboard from Mrs Bomberger's room.

"The reason why each of these people was so deeply concerned was that, however Mrs Bomberger may have died, almost everyone had planned, or intended, or hoped to kill her. Gracie Stayer had bought an arsenical weed poison which she intended to use when occasion offered. Graveston had persuaded Mrs Bomberger to be pushed in her bath-chair every afternoon to the clifftop, from which it would be easy, on the right day of low visibility, to let the chair run over the cliff.

"Ron Cribb had the most ingenious plan. He had discovered that the cable of his hand-brake ran under his battery, so that by over-filling his battery with distilled water he could cause the acid from it to fall on the brake-cable and slowly, naturally, eat it away. No one examining it after any accident could suggest that it had been deliberately cut or frayed, yet when the moment came and there was only a strand left, he could put on the hand-brake apparently quite securely, get out of the car, give it a shove from behind and watch it run over the edge of the cliff with Lillianne Bomberger inside it. It is an old gag for murder, but it works every time unless it can be proved that the driver omitted to put on his hand-brake.

"Moreover, every one of them had plenty of motive. Lillianne Bomberger was a much-hated woman, particularly in her own household, and to each of them she had behaved abominably, even to Gloria Cribb, whose child she resented. Ron Cribb she had reduced to bitterness by making him economically dependent, a position which his wife, with a growing son, would not let him escape. She had come between Babs Stayer and the man she wanted to marry, she had bullied and humiliated Gracie, Miss Pink and Graveston, who were all tied to her by the mysterious dominion she had obtained over their wills. And to all of them she was known to have left money.

"So when Lillianne was found dead the whole household was scared and guilty and conferred on what should be done. Only the murderer or murderess knew the cause of her death—the rest were half thankful that it wasn't through his or her particular line, half fearful that they might even so be blamed.

"But someone at that conference, someone who had particular cause to be afraid, was strong-minded. In half an hour this person had persuaded them all, waverers and cowards and all, that they did not dare leave her body in the house, that *any one* of them might be accused of murder with previous attempts or plans as supporting evidence, and that the only hope was to get the body out of the house and make Mrs Bomberger's death appear the work of someone not in the household. This person probably used as arguments that a phone call from an unknown man had come through that night, that George Stump had called . . ."

"Ha! ha!" said Mr Gorringer derisively.

"And that there was actually a novel of Mrs Bomberger's called *Life Has Death For Neighbour* in which a woman murdered by her husband was found on the beach. People, particularly people with a guilty conscience, are not at their most strong-minded when woken at two o'clock in the morning. In the end this person, who had a particular reason for wanting it, succeeded in persuading the rest and they got to work.

"Two or more of the women went up and dressed the body in one of the dead woman's most elaborate gowns. Then she was carried to her bath-chair. I do not pretend to know exactly which members of the household went down to the shore, but certainly Graveston did with a spade that already and legitimately bore his finger-prints, certainly Gracie Stayer in her black velvet shoes, probably Babs Stayer, who took the precaution of wearing beach shoes, I imagine Ron Cribb, because as a man he could assist Graveston. Miss Pink and Gloria Cribb may have stayed behind. We shall know that in due course."

"How?" asked Detective Inspector Whibley with a smile.

"Because when faced with the truth now one of the four survivors of that night will break down and tell you what happened. I, thank heavens, shall be a long way away."

Mr. Gorringer cleared his throat.

"I feel," he said, "that that is a signal for us to give Deene a little break from his exhausting task. Detective Inspector, may I offer you some refreshment?"

"Thank you. I'll have a lager beer."

"I hope the young lady downstairs can supply it. We will see. You doubtless find Deene's exposition of interest?"

"There's very little so far which we did not know or suspect."

"Ah! For once the private investigator and the official police are in agreement. That is indeed a break from precedent."

"There's a long way to go yet," warned Whibley.

Bomberger was seen to approach George Stump.

"I say, old man, is that right you're one of the executors?"

"I am."

"I'm her husband, you know. Otto Bomberger. Can you tell me if there's anything for me in the will?"

"I prefer not to discuss it at present."

"Oh, come on, old man. You can't do that, you know. It means a lot to me. You must remember whether I'm in or not?"

"I will go so far as to say that I *do* seem to remember a sum being left to Otto Bomberger. Yes."

"Do you really, old man? How much was it?"

"Silence, please," said Mr Gorringer. "Deene is now ready to continue his most lucid . . . er . . . discourse."

"So Lillianne Bomberger's body was taken to a part of the sands which would be covered by several feet of water when the tide came in and buried there. It was almost directly opposite the house, the nearest point they could find. There was no attempt to forestall a discovery of the body—on the contrary, it was intended to be found next day. A deep enough hole was dug to bury her standing with her head protruding and she was lowered into it. The party then returned to the house, so far as we know unobserved.

"Then these people, who had no experience of crime, set about, in a very foolish and amateurish way, to eliminate the evidence of what they had done. They thought the glasses from which they had drunk during their conference would show that there had been a conference and carefully cleared them away and washed them up, cleaning out the ash-trays. They did not realize that this would be in itself suspicious and, characteristically, they forgot to lock up the drinks cupboard and return the key to Mrs Bomberger's room. They knew that the sand and damp on the wheels of the bath-chair would be evidence that it had been down to the beach, but did not see that a noticeably clean bath-chair would call attention to itself. They arranged that all should have the same story, that they had gone to bed at eleven—in the cases of Alice Pink and Graveston rather later—and had heard nothing during the night, but they forgot to invent details for the morning. And so on.

"From then onwards it was obvious that they were frightened and guilty people. Even my cousin noticed it and was sorry for them. They agreed to my being sent for because they thought that in some mysterious way I could protect them from the police.

"I had another reason, which I do not propose to give now, for knowing that something had happened on the beach that night which the people at Trumbles had to conceal at all costs."

Carolus carefully avoided looking towards Poxton. Whatever he felt about the man, he had given his word.

"I noticed, too, that they all made the most of the two events that night which were not concerned with them—the phone call from a stranger calling himself Green and Mr George Stump's late call at the house. Finally there was Gracie Stayer's slip of the tongue. In reply to a question as to whether the beach would be deserted that night she said, "There was no one about." She tried to cover this by adding, "There can have been no one about. We should have heard. It would have come out at the inquest." But the harm was done. One way or another, though I had no more than circumstantial evidence, I was pretty sure that I knew how and by whom and when Lillianne Bomberger was buried.

"But that was not to say I knew the details of her death. I was convinced it wasn't suicide."

"Why?" again put in Whibley disconcertingly.

"She was not a woman to commit suicide. In her appallingly selfish way she enjoyed life and enjoyed making other people miserable. She believed, like many of the most second-rate writers, that she was a great one. She had no reason to commit suicide. She was enjoying her row with George Stump. That very afternoon she had been— heaven save us—to the Spanish Patio of the Royal Hydro Hotel to an orchestral tea, or something of the sort. She was in a particularly good mood that evening. She had arranged by telephone to see her husband next day. No. Lillianne certainly did not mean to kill herself."

"She was murdered, then?" asked George Stump calmly.

"Yes. But before going into that I should like to pass on to the death of Alice Pink."

There was a gasp, partly of exasperation, partly of tense interest, which went through the room.

"Alice Pink became rather odd after Mrs Bomberger's death. She took to drinking spirits, which she had never done to anyone's knowledge before."

"Certainly not," put in her sister. "I can scarcely believe it of her now. She knew very well I would never put up with nonsense like that. I don't like it in men, let alone women."

"But there is evidence that she did. She also formed a habit of walking up to the shelter on the cliff in the evening and eating sandwiches there rather than dine with Babs and Gracie Stayer. It seems likely that on one afternoon she almost made up her mind to commit suicide and went so far as to type a letter saying what she was doing, but repented of it and returned to the house. On the same day, if Mrs Plum's evidence is correct, she gave the impression that she was going to reveal what she knew.

"Then, on the afternoon of a misty day, she tried to reach me by telephone and left a message saying that she was coming to see me next day at a time when her absence would not be noticed. On the same evening she took her usual walk and never returned from it. Her body was found half-way down the cliff. She had been murdered. Later an autopsy revealed the same poison as the one which killed Mrs Bomberger."

"But why poison, Deene?" boomed Mr Gorringer. "That is the inexplicable thing. If someone murdered this unfortunate lady by pushing her over the cliff, why was it necessary to administer poison? Or were two people determined to kill her?"

"Nobody murdered Alice Pink by pushing her over the cliff. That is the whole point. Surely you must see that it would be virtually an impossibility? And if it were attempted it would mean grave risk to the murderer. You try pushing someone over a cliff, someone active and wiry like Alice Pink. How would you get her to the edge, in the first place? And if you were large and powerful enough to achieve that, do you think she would remain silent? Her screams would have been heard for half a mile in that mist. And once there, how would you push her over without her trying to drag you over, and perhaps succeed in doing so? She wouldn't be walking conveniently on the cliff edge on a misty night waiting for someone to rush up and shove her over. It's all very well to talk glibly about murdering people by pushing them over a cliff, but in all the history of crime have you ever known it happen? Cliffs have been used, yes, but always to dispose of the body in a doubly convenient way, for if the victim was battered to death before being thrown over it would probably be impossible to distinguish between the two kinds of injury. That is altogether another matter. A person in his full senses and with the use of his limbs could not be murdered in that way; that is why I immediately suggested that the intestines in this case should be examined. No, somebody poisoned Alice Pink and when she was dead rolled her body down the slight slope from the shelter to the cliff and over its edge. It was intended to look like suicide."

20

"IT is exactly as I said." Ethel Pink spoke loudly and decisively. "My sister was murdered because she knew too much."

"Not so much that," said Carolus, "as that she was about to reveal it to me. Surely we may take it that the knowledge she had would incriminate the murderer of Mrs Bomberger. I mean, a murder to silence someone (at least among normally non-criminal people) would scarcely be undertaken unless silence was a matter of life and death. So the murderer of Mrs Bomberger poisoned Alice Pink and rolled her body over the cliff to prevent her giving me a piece of information which would both identify and prove the case against him or her.

"The field is narrowing now. In a moment I am going to give the name of the murderer, and when I do so some of you will immediately say, 'I knew it all along'. But you won't really be speaking the truth, you know. What you'll mean is that the person named is *one* of those who, at different times during this thing, you have suspected. If you *knew* who was the murderer, you would have known how the murders were committed. You could not know one without the other.

"We are faced then with the necessity of finding a person who fits a number of qualifications. Who had a motive for murdering Mrs Bomberger and seeing that she was buried in the sand where the tide would cover her. Who could persuade the rest of those concerned to carry this out. Who knew that Alice Pink was going to tell me something incriminating. Who had an opportunity of poisoning Alice Pink's flask. Who could have been out on the cliff on the night of Alice Pink's murder. One would suppose that these must limit the choice to one or at the most two people, but on the contrary they do nothing of the sort. At least five people fit them all: Gracie Stayer, Babs Stayer, Ron Cribb, Gloria Cribb, Graveston—it could have been any of these. It could conceivably have been one of those in the outer ring of suspects—George Stump or Primmley, for instance.

"I'll try to let you see how I arrived at it. I went back to the very core of the thing, and remembered afresh that Mrs Bomberger had died from swallowing six sleeping-pills when two or three would have been fatal. Alice Pink in her letter to her sister said, 'It was I who gave Mrs Bomberger her sleeping-pills that night.' Was Alice Pink the murderer, then? *Yes, unless she did not know that those six pills would be fatal.* It was then that the thing flashed home. Everything was accounted for: the suddenly increased consumption of Komatoza, the availability of morphine poisoning for Alice Pink (a point which had troubled me a great deal)—everything fell beautifully into place.

"Mrs Bomberger was not killed by an overdose so much as by a long period of underdoses. I remembered something said by Gracie Stayer which made an instant impression on me. She was speaking of the Komatoza tablets taken by her and Babs—'we sometimes believed they were just as good as Aunt Lillianne's, though they were a tenth of the price. *They looked the same, anyway.*'

"I doubt if Mrs Bomberger, until the night of her death, took more than one or two of the sleeping-tablets prescribed for her by Dr Flitcher. I don't see how she can have. According to Mr Cupperly there were twenty tablets in each box, and only two boxes were supplied. From the second box she took the six that killed her, while the remaining fourteen were at once removed by the police, of course. From the first box there were enough left to kill Alice Pink and Babs Stayer, so if Mrs Bomberger ever had any of them, it was very few. What she took was Komatoza, increasing her doses until she had reached the total of six. Komatoza, which 'looked the same'. Komatoza put in the box supplied for her prescribed pills. Until one night when everything was ready for it, when there were six possible murderers in the house, when a strange phone call had come and George Stump, with whom Lillianne was quarrelling, had called—on this night instead of Komatoza was put the real thing. 'I'll take six,' Mrs Bomberger may have said to Miss Pink, whom she had called. Perhaps Miss Pink protested against the number. 'Nonsense,' one imagines Mrs Bomberger saying. 'I *often* take six.' Which was true when they were Komatoza. These killed her, of course.

"It was the murderer who went to her room and found she was dead. It was the murderer who, though well covered by the fact that Mrs Bomberger had taken an overdose of her own free will and *not* in the murderer's presence, yet felt that it might be safer to let the tide go over Mrs Bomberger and—the murderer believed— eliminate all trace of poison from the intestines. It was the murderer who persuaded the others, therefore, to undertake that extraordinary form of burial. . . ."

"Oh, come on, sir," said Priggley impatiently. "You're twisting yourself into knots trying to avoid mentioning the name or even use a masculine or feminine pronoun. Who was it?"

"Babs Stayer," said Carolus, and was silent.

There was general relief when Mr Gorringer again, and with a cavernous rumbling, cleared his throat.

"Let us once again allow Deene to relax for a few moments. I'm sure that the strain must be a telling one."

The waiter was summoned and a few drinks ordered, but the gathering remained subdued. The only person to move was Otto Bomberger, who again crossed to where George Stump was sitting.

"Look here, old man, this is a serious matter. It means a great deal to me. Surely you can remember how much it was she left me?"

183

George Stump raised his hand.

"Not now. Not now," he said solemnly. "This is not the moment."

"It is for me," said Bomberger. "It couldn't be a better moment for me. Would it have been five hundred, would you say?"

"You will hear in due course."

Mrs Plum could repress herself no longer.

"There!" she said, "what did I tell you? It's enough to make anyone sign the pledge, isn't it? I feel giddy like, as though the room was going round. That Babs, the sly thing, murdering her auntie like that. No wonder they wanted to get rid of me. You can't wonder at it, can you? I could scream when I remember it. And to think of me working in that house! How I escaped with a whole skin I *don't* know!"

"Hush," said Mr Gorringer. "Deene, we're all agog."

"I said that many people had a motive for murdering Lillianne Bomberger, and it was true. There never was such a natural-born murderee. But those were the muddled motives of hatred and greed which produced muddled schemes and hopes. Babs had a fierce and urgent motive which produced a clever plan. When I asked her *how* her aunt could prevent her marrying the man she loved, she spoke indefinitely about her aunt. 'She would find a way' were Babs' words, but I was pretty sure that Lillianne had already found a way. When I received information that there was inherited lunacy in the family I perceived what this way was. Mrs Bomberger was blackmailing her niece by threatening to tell her fiancé this fact. It is probably the only one which can be guaranteed to break off an engagement at once.

"After motive—opportunity. Who had better? It was she who took the prescription to Cupperly, she who received Cupperly's warning about the pills, she who noticed their similarity in appearance to Komatoza. I do not know whether she started by giving Mrs Bomberger one or two of the prescribed pills and then, relying on the psychology of self-persuasion, filled her box with Komatoza, or whether she started with Komatoza from the first. At all events she put Komatoza tablets in place of the prescribed ones, then encouraged Mrs Bomberger to increase the number she took until it was five or six. Thus the Komatoza consumption in the house rose steeply, as Cupperly said it did.

"Babs kept in her own possession the prescribed pills and used them later, as we shall see. Meanwhile, everything was prepared for the night on which Mrs Bomberger was to kill herself. Babs kept carefully away from her room that night, but unexpectedly Mrs Bomberger sent for Miss Pink and told her to give her the pills. This was unfortunate. It meant that Miss Pink's evidence could be dangerous. For a woman who takes a fatal dose, *knowing it to be one*, is scarcely likely to call someone else in to give it her, or to say on the phone, as she did to her husband, 'Come tomorrow because I have just taken my sleeping-pills'. That 'S' on pills when Bomberger told me his wife had spoken of her sleeping-pills, instead of the one pill she was supposed to take, I thought was one of the most useful bits of information I had at the time.

"I feel pretty confident that it was Babs who went to Mrs Bomberger's room during the night and found her dead, but of course she may have been subtle enough to cause someone else to go. I even wondered whether Alice Pink's 'voice on the wind' may have been a device to get her to make the discovery, but that is far-fetched.

"Then came the toughest job for Babs: to frighten and persuade everyone to carry out her purpose. It was interesting that each of them had had a scheme for killing Mrs Bomberger but that only Babs had to put it into operation, yet Babs over-ruled all their objections and got the thing done as she wanted it. I think she believed that all trace of poison would be out of the body after some hours in water. In that case Mrs Bomberger would appear to have been drowned, and whoever could be blamed for that she, Babs Stayer, could not be. She had her second line of defence if the poison was discovered, for there was no way of proving that she had juggled the two kinds of sleeping-pills.

"On the whole she succeeded fairly well. When the body was buried they all felt thoroughly guilty, and I shouldn't be surprised if Babs pointed out that they were all accessories now. They, on the other hand, had no reason to suspect Babs and were pleased with her lead and confidence.

"Everybody came down late next morning, including Graveston, whose snoring Mrs Plum heard after nine o'clock. But even that did not seem to matter for a while until I began asking awkward questions about it. The bath-chair, Gracie's shoes—none of these seemed very important. Mrs Bomberger was safely dead and nobody had an inkling of how it had happened.

"In fact the first thing that began to worry Babs was the behaviour of Alice Pink. The secretary was the only one who had felt, mixed with her fear and hatred of Mrs Bomberger, some kind of twisted affection for her. After her death Miss Pink became very peculiar in her manner and was caught helping herself to gin. She almost broke down under my cross-examination more than once, but Babs had drilled into her, I am sure, how dangerous was her situation as the one who had actually administered the poison, and she held out.

"Whether Babs knew that Alice Pink was coming to me next day to tell me all she knew, or whether she just took advantage of a misty night, we cannot know. I think the latter. I think she had persuaded Graveston to follow Alice on several occasions on these evening walks. Indeed Graveston almost admitted as much, contradicting Babs, who said he had *once* seen Alice Pink in the shelter. I think Babs had decided that the emotional Alice Pink who longed to tell the truth and knew that Mrs Bomberger had swallowed six sleeping-pills without realizing their certain effect, was too dangerous a person to live.

"It was very easy to kill her. A few of the morphine sleeping-tablets (kept from the first packet unused by Mrs Bomberger) dissolved in the contents of Miss Pink's flask would be sufficient to kill or perhaps just render her unconscious. Babs 'discovered' her absence soon after she left, followed her up to the shelter on the plea of finding and looking after her, waited till the morphine had had its effect and rolled the dead or nearly dead body over the edge of the cliff. Then she returned and with all security sent out search-parties to look for her.

"If Mrs Plum's story is true about a projected suicide by Alice Pink some days earlier, with a note left on her typewriter taken while she was out . . ."

"What do you mean 'if it's true'?" asked Mrs Plum indignantly. "If you had seen what I've seen in that house all you'd wonder is that it wasn't worse. I wake up in the night all of a sweat and a shiver when I think of it, and you'd do the same if you knew the half of it. Of course it's true."

"Then it is possible that Babs kept that note as a sort of insurance. After all, she could appear to find it at any moment among the dead woman's papers. It may even still be there. But it doesn't matter much.

"At this point the case was clear in my mind. I had no proof—indeed I haven't now any proof acceptable to a court of law—but I am sufficiently sure to count on evidence which can be obtained from Miss Gracie Stayer, from Graveston and from Mr and Mrs Cribb which will confirm the whole story.* I did not see how there could be proof unless Miss Gracie Stayer could be frightened or persuaded into giving evidence against her sister. That piece of investigation, on those lines, I was not prepared to undertake. It was work for the police, not for me. So I decided to throw in my hand.

"Before doing so, however, I let Babs Stayer know that I

---

* Carolus was right here. At his next interview with these persons Detective Inspector Whibley obtained the whole truth, which, with certain trifling differences, was as Carolus supposed.

was aware of the truth. At an interview with the family I said, 'Both murders were ingenious and lucky, and it may be that no charge will be brought until the police obtain a certain piece of evidence which I do not wish to obtain. Please don't ask me what it is, for if I answered that I should be revealing more than I ought. I will say only that it *can* be obtained, that it almost certainly will be, but that it is not for me to obtain it.' Moreover I told the members of the family that I should tell the police what I knew, if they needed it. Babs became perfectly aware that she was in mortal danger. It was too late now to try to close more mouths, or I haven't the slightest doubt that she would have killed her sister. Instead of that she committed suicide. I have nothing more to say."

In the buzz of awed chatter which succeeded this Mr Gorringer approached Whibley.

"Well, Inspector, what do you make of that? You won't deny it was a brilliant exposition, I'm sure?"

"I won't deny anything," said Whibley with his usual good humour. "On the other hand, I can admit nothing, I'm afraid. The police cannot give 'brilliant expositions', as you term it. They work at a case like this without explaining to all and sundry what their conclusions may be. I cannot tell you with how much of what Mr Deene has said I agree or disagree or how much was known to me already. I will say that I was extremely interested."

"Ah, that is a concession!" said Mr Gorringer, delighted. "Deene, my dear fellow, you deserve a drink. Oh, but I see you have one already."

"You seem to find it all very cheering, headmaster," said Carolus bitterly.

Mr Gorringer at once assumed an air of solemnity.

"It is a terrible affair, Deene. Terrible. Two murders and a suicide. I am appalled. My only consolation is that my publisher, Mr George Stump, is in no way involved, as I feared from your earlier, somewhat flippant, remarks he might be. That and the fact that through coming here at this time I have been able to replace Mrs Critchley, our school matron, so very appropriately. I have no doubt that Miss Ethel Pink will be a treasure. A treasure."

Across the room Mr Stump was almost held in his chair by Otto Bomberger.

"But you can't have forgotten, old man. It's not a thing you can have forgotten, like that. Think of its importance to me. Now cast your mind back. What sort of sum . . ."

"It is a thousand pounds," snapped George Stump in exasperation.

"Is it, by Jove? That's not so bad. It might have been more, of course."

"It might have been considerably less," said Stump and at last got himself away.

It was Mrs Plum, however, who had the last word.

"It only shows, doesn't it? She might have gone on one after another if she hadn't decided to do for herself. It's enough to turn anyone to drink and the horrors to think o. it. And you're going away, are you?" she asked Carolus. "Well, I suppose you can now you've told us all about it. I don't suppose it'll please her where you've been staying to know that her house has been mixed up in anything like this, but there you are. I'm glad if anything I've said has been of help, but I couldn't have kept it to myself, not if you were to have offered me a fortune. I should never have been able to sleep at night."

"That seems to have been a common complaint," said Priggley. "You should try reading *The Wayward* . . ."

"Priggley," said Carolus irritably and silenced him.

Within an hour Carolus, taking his cousin with him, had thankfully left the town.

"A beastly case," was all he ever said about it.

THE END